Weapon
of
Opportunity

Kiernan Kelly

WEAPON OF OPPORTUNITY
An imprint of Evil Plot Bunny, LLC
PO Box 722
Loughman, FL 33837
Copyright © 2009 by Kiernan Kelly
Cover by Kiernan Kelly
Published with permission
ISBN: 978-1951777-14-2
www.evilplotbunny.com
First Printing: April 2011
Second Edition: January 2020
Printed in the USA

Dedication: For my husband, my most diehard supporter, for knowing when to crack the whip and when to salve the wounds. Thank you, hon. For my family, for knowing when to tread lightly and when to strike up the band. Most of all, for my readers, without whom there would be no point at all.

Prologue

In his dreams, he can fly.

Perched twelve stories above the busy city street, the toes of his bare feet edging past the lip of the rooftop, Cooper spreads his arms and smiles. Night has fallen in the world outside his bedroom walls, but the sun is always shining in his dreams. There is no reason to close his eyes. He *wants* to see the street fly up to meet him, to see the blacktop whiz by as he levels off, his body barely skimming the macadam.

A strong wind buffets him as he leans forward and steps off into empty air. He swoops down for several stories before shooting upward in a graceful arc, higher and higher, until he feels the sun heat his skin and the cloud's cool condensation salve the burn. He finds himself in the midst of a flock of geese flying in tight formation, and levels off, assuming the lead position for several minutes. They accept him unquestioningly as one of their own, honking a greeting.

When he sees the perimeter of the city approaching, the suspension bridge glistening like a green, dew-kissed spider web bridging the river, he veers off from the flock. Diving sharply, he finds himself again between the soaring skyscrapers, smiling at his reflection in their tinted windows. He flies lower still, until he surfs the air just above the few pedestrians' heads, close enough to ruffle the hair of the tallest of them.

No one sees him. Cooper is like the wind, invisible but tangible at the same time. The people can feel him, like the brush of a breeze against their cheeks, but don't consciously acknowledge his presence. That, at least, is no different from his waking life. He feels invisible there too, except to his Mama and sometimes to Bobby. It's never a good thing when Bobby notices him. Bobby scares him.

He shrugs off the stray, frightening thought, intent on enjoying his freedom while it lasts. That's when he hears it.

A scream, sharp and shrill, cuts through his bones and makes his teeth ache. He falters, nearly plummeting to the hard ground below.

The scream terrifies him. The sound is full of pain and fear, contagious and overwhelming. He tries, but is incapable of ignoring it, unable wake and return to his bed. It calls to him like a siren's song, snatching at him like a tyrant's hand, forcing him to obey.

Cooper unerringly flies down one street and up another as if following an unseen map. He turns at a corner, heading south, and then west. Finally, he reaches a narrow alleyway between two older buildings. One is in the process of being refurbished; it's been bared to its wooden stud bones, with only a few broken sections of plaster walls remaining, like the desiccated skin of a corpse stubbornly clinging to its skeleton. Cooper thinks he might recognize the place; it isn't far from his home. Though the buildings might be familiar, strange smells and sounds fill the air.

Two figures struggle in the narrow space between a pair of small Dumpsters below him in the alley. One person is dressed in a black overcoat, even though the weather is warm. The other wears a T-shirt and jeans.

Unable to stop himself, Cooper dips lower, hovering just above the pair like a small dark-haired angel clad in Power Ranger pajamas. He notices a third figure, an older woman, brown hair streaked with gray, dressed in a flowered housecoat and fluffy pink slippers, standing at the mouth of the alley. The woman pauses, glances at the action going on inside the alley, then hurries away down the street.

The fight continues as another person, an old man pushing a squeaking shopping cart, pauses in front of the alley. Cooper can feel his fear crackling in the air before he scuttles away into the dark.

Cooper turns his full attention back to the men who are fighting.

The larger man, the one in the black coat, is holding a length of white pipe in his hand. Raising it high in the air, he brings it down on the smaller man's head with a sickening *crunch*.

Again.

And again, even though the smaller man lies crumpled on the ground.

"Stop!" Cooper shouts, unable to bear the sound of the pipe striking the poor man's skull one more time. His heart is hammering in his narrow chest, pulse pounding in his ears, his body shivering as a cold sweat drenches him. He's terrified; he wants his mother and the security of his room, to be tucked under the covers of his bed, but is too frightened to move.

To his astonishment, the man with the pipe pauses and looks up, meeting Cooper's horrified eyes with a cold, black gaze. The left side of the stranger's face is hideous, pitted with black burns that go bone deep; his lip curls in a sneer.

Cooper is thunderstruck, realizing that the man can *see* him. No one *ever* sees Cooper in his dreams except… His shock is enough to drop him from the air like a stone, and he hits the pavement on his hands and knees with enough force to knock the breath out of him.

Cooper's lungs inadvertently gulp air and expel it in a scream when the man with the white pipe turns toward him. He can smell the blood that's splashed on the man's coat and the pipe; it smells like old, wet pennies gone green with age.

He feels the familiar pull in his belly without warning, like a rope suddenly pulled taut. It yanks him away, but he barely has the time to feel relief. In an instant, he's safe, back inside his house, wide awake. He's huddled on the floor in a corner of the living room between the sofa and the lace-draped drum table, shaking like a leaf, crying; snot mixes with tears in a sticky mess on his face. Bringing his knees to his chest, he screws his eyes shut tightly, desperately trying to rid himself of the remnants of his dream, uncaring that in his terror, he's wet himself.

Rocking back and forth in the corner, Cooper doesn't notice that his knees and palms are bleeding, as if he's skinned them in a fall.

Chapter One

"Fuck you."

"Not likely, although I do admit I love it when you talk dirty to me," David's humor was as dry as white toast. "Come on, Hunter. You know you owe me."

"I don't know anything of the sort. What I *do* know is that you're a jackass with more dick than brains. Oh wait. You don't have either one, do you?" Hunter could be surpremely snide when the occasion called for it.

"Asshole."

"In case you haven't noticed, you seem to be lacking one of those too. Amazing how you can spew so much shit without one, though."

"Oh now that was just hurtful, Hunter. My body may be insubstantial, but I'm every bit as aesthetically pleasing as I was before." David huffed, and turned his back in a snit. "All parts are present and accounted for, and you know it." It really irritated him when Hunter made him beg. It wasn't as if David had any other option, and Hunter damn well knew it. David had *earned* the right to hitchhike on occasion -- that was the deal they'd made after all. David had held up his end of the bargain, and he wished Hunter would stop trying to renege.

Okay, so maybe Hunter hadn't actually *agreed* to it, but he'd accepted David's help in the past, and that amounted to the same thing, didn't it? He would have thought that as a cop, Hunter would be above petty thievery. As far as David was concerned, it was no different from downloading unlicensed music and books from the Internet. Hunter was pirating David's assistance without paying for it, and that was just plain wrong.

"Come on, Hunter. It's been *forever*..." David cringed at the whiny sound of his own voice. Damn it! He *hated* to beg, but it had been months since the last time, and he was getting desperate. Never mind "getting"...he was past desperate and halfway to frantic. If he'd *had* actual balls, they'd be blue by now. When Hunter didn't respond, he gave him his back again.

"Sulk all you want." Hunter shrugged into his jacket. "I'm not going to tell you again, David. Stay out of my head."

"Which head -- the big fat one on the end of your neck, or the tiny one three feet lower?"

"Both," Hunter snipped. "Oh and for the record, if the lower one was *tiny*, I'll bet you wouldn't be hounding me all the time!" The door slammed shut behind him like an exclamation point on the end of their conversation as he stalked out of the apartment.

David stared at the closed door for a long moment. Hunter could be an arrogant prick, hardboiled, callous, and totally unsympathetic at times to David's plight, but underneath it all, David knew Hunter had a warm heart and a compassionate soul.

Maybe not *compassionate* per se, David thought. More like tolerant. Sometimes. Once in a while. On occasion.

A slow smile spread across David's face as he slipped out of the apartment, out into the street. *Tonight is going to be one of those occasions, whether Hunter thinks it will or not.* His grin grew wider and lecherous. *He's going to get laid. I can smell it. He just doesn't know it yet.*

There were damn few advantages to not having a pulse, but the ability to manipulate space was one of the most useful. David had come to realize over time that space was like a blanket. Spread out evenly, it created a large area that took time and effort to traverse. Folded up tightly, it took up a lot less room and David, as one of the dearly departed, had the ability to press it into accordion pleats, if he so desired. He could travel from one end of the city to the other in practically no time. It'd taken years of practice to master the skill. David had suffered through many mishaps along the way -- reappearing halfway between walls, floors, and on one memorable occasion, on a set of railroad tracks just before the eight o'clock commuter train rocketed by -- but it'd all been worth it for the ability to pop in and out of anywhere at will.

Sometimes being a ghost had its merits.

Truthfully, David hated the term "ghost." It reminded him of himself as a kid, running around draped in his mother's crisp, white linen sheets on Halloween, eyeholes cut out crookedly, the toes of his Keds peeking out from underneath. And *that* reminded him of the smell of tart apples and cinnamon, and the taste of chocolate, and a myriad of other half-remembered pleasures that had become merely ghosts themselves.

Sex being chief among them.

God, he missed sex most of all. Missed it more than a frosty beer fresh from the tap; even more than a hand-rolled Cuban, or a thick, rare hamburger swimming in fried onions and grease. Hell, he missed sex more than he missed breathing.

Luckily, David had discovered a secret that few -- if any -- of the Incorporeal Club, as he often thought of the others who shared his deceased status, knew existed. Or if they did, they kept it as closely guarded a secret as he did. Given the right person, a psychic or someone with a strong sense of empathy, a ghost could live vicariously through them for a short time, feeling emotions and physical sensations just as sharply and powerfully as when he'd been alive.

David had found that person in Hunter, who possessed a strong empathic streak, although Hunter would never admit to it. They also shared another connection that went bone deep; one that was profound enough to bridge the gap between the living and the dead, and helped ease the way for David to tap into Hunter's emotions. The bond had been formed when David had been alive -- they'd been partners and close friends for eleven years. That was back when they were Detectives David Brown and Hunter Vance of the Third Precinct, before David was gunned down in the line of duty. Closer than brothers, Hunter had mourned David's death for a full year.

David wasn't sure why their connection enabled Hunter to see and hear David when no other living person he'd come across -- so far, at least -- could, and as far as David knew, Hunter couldn't see any other ghosts…just David. He figured it was because of their close bond during life, but quite frankly, he didn't care. Nobody really cared why or how television worked; only that it *did*, and you didn't miss the latest episode of your favorite show.

Nowadays, Hunter spent most of their time together trying to get *rid* of David, not that David would ever considering leaving. The only alternative to living -- for lack of a better term -- a half-life *with* Hunter was enduring none at all *without* him. It was no option, as far as David was concerned.

Christening his discovery "hitchhiking," David indulged himself in it fully and at every possible opportunity. Sadly, such times were few and far between with Hunter, especially when it came to sex.

The man was an absolute control freak when it came to his feelings. Hunter rarely let loose, or allowed himself to feel passionate enough about something for David to tap into his emotions, and worse, he barely *ever* got laid. David knew Hunter was never one to hang out at clubs, and he couldn't recall Hunter ever having had a relationship lasting more than a few months at most, but he didn't remember him being exactly virginal, either. It seemed to David that Hunter's sex life had gone from spotty to scarce to nearly nonexistent after David's death.

It wasn't his looks. Hunter would be virtually stunning if he ever lost the boxy, off-the-rack, hopelessly outdated, rumpled suits he wore, and discovered hair care products. Topping six feet two, Hunter kept his body in great shape, working out as frequently as his schedule allowed. He was thirty-seven years old, but was aging incredibly well. The combination of his broad shoulders, trim waist, and an ass that men ten years younger would kill to possess made for an incredibly attractive hunk of man. His eyes were the most piercing green David could ever remember seeing, clear and expressive, set in a face that was almost movie-star handsome. Hunter's only flaws were a slightly crooked nose that'd been broken one time too many, and a disposition that could curdle milk.

The former added character to Hunter's face, in David's opinion. The latter was what kept his bed empty and cold most of the time, which in turn, resulted in the rarity of David's sexual hitchhiking opportunities.

Not tonight. David had gleaned a nugget of information from Hunter's brain that was very encouraging. Hunter was going to Feathers, a bar not far from the precinct. There was only one reason for him to go to one of the most notorious gay bars in the city, and it had *nothing* to do with the two-for-one drink specials and *everything* to do with the thick piece of meat hanging between Hunter's thighs.

Hunter was going cruising, even if he wouldn't admit it to himself, and he was going to have a hitchhiker with him whether he wanted one or not.

David was still smiling as he slipped through the outer wall of Hunter's apartment. He was immediately enveloped in what felt like thick cotton candy, the oddly soft sensation caused by folding space. He emerged on the sidewalk outside of the apartment building a second or two later. There was Hunter's green piece-of-shit Dodge, just pulling away from the curb. David arched an eyebrow and sighed. He needed to have a serious talk with Hunter about getting a better ride. Most people wouldn't be caught dead in that ugly tin-can-on-wheels. As with everything else about his appearance, Hunter simply didn't seem to give a shit.

Another quick burst of energy, and David found himself riding shotgun.

"Hey, babe. Miss me?" he asked, laughing when Hunter gasped and nearly sideswiped a cab as his hands jerked the steering wheel in surprise.

"What the fuck are you doing here? How many times do I have to tell you not to do that popping-in-and-out thing?" Hunter snarled, shooting a black look in David's direction.

"Speaking of popping in and out, we *are* going to get some tonight, right?" David asked, ignoring both of Hunter's questions.

"That's none of your fucking business. I told you to stay out of my head. Get out!"

"Not a chance. I helped you solve the Grayson case, remember? Being in that sicko's head was *not* fun. You *owe* me." It was the truth. Grayson was a serial killer who delighted in torturing his victims to death. Getting inside his head had been like wading nose-deep in the foulest shithole in hell. It was worth it in the end, since David was able to pick the killer's brain for information that eventually resulted in Hunter's apprehension of the sick bastard, but he still got the heebie-jeebies thinking about the case.

"I don't get it, David. You were as straight as a fucking two-by-four when you were alive. I'm into men, and I always have been. Before you died, I couldn't even *mention* my dates to you without you gagging and turning green. Now you want in their pants more than I do. What gives?"

Wow. Was that an actual, intelligent question instead of the usual grunt or snarl? Should he tell Hunter the truth? Nah, he wasn't ready to hear it yet. David decided to hedge a little, give a half-truth rather than freak Hunter out with reality and lose any opportunity he might have for a hitchhiked orgasm.

"Are you sure you really want to know? Okay, but don't say I didn't warn you. After you die, the whole gay/straight thing becomes kind of a moot point since the dead don't have sex, Hunter. I'm the only exception to the rule that I'm aware of, and while even *I* don't have sex in the purest sense of the word, an orgasm is an orgasm. Now that I've discovered the secret, I'll take one any way I can get one. So far, since the only way I've found I can feel a climax is if *you* get your jollies, it means I've officially jumped the fence."

"I'm sorry I asked."

"I knew you would be, but it doesn't matter anyway. You still owe me, *partner*."

David could practically hear Hunter's molars grinding. He had Hunter by the balls, and Hunter knew it. "Fine, but put some clothes on, will ya? I'm going blind, here."

Aw, shit. He'd forgotten again. The dead tended to shed their inhibitions at the same time they shed their fleshy remains. Since they didn't feel cold, heat, and very little in the way of embarrassment, they really had no reason to bother manifesting clothing. For some reason, Hunter was less than enthusiastic at having David running about in all his natural wonder. David could never quite figure out the why of it, either, considering Hunter was into men. If Hunter were straight, then David could've understood it, but what gay man wouldn't enjoy his own private peepshow following him around?

No one, that's who…except for Hunter.

There's nothing wrong with my body, either, except for being slightly less than alive. Oh, and there's the hole in my chest where I was shot, but other than that one teeny, tiny flaw, I'm a hottie. Maybe it's the "former partner" thing. Yeah, that must be it.

Nonetheless, he flashed on the approximation of a pair of jeans, a long-sleeved T-shirt, and a pair of snakeskin boots. His clothing was an illusion; the threads no more substantial than he was, which was another benefit as far as David was concerned. He could dress in Armani or a Savile Row suit whenever he pleased without the irksome tailoring or snide looks from the clerks when the bank declined his credit card.

"There. Better? Happy? Good. Now let's go find us a piece of ass, okay?" he said, reaching for the radio. Of course, his hand passed through the radio into the dashboard. "We're not on radio silence, Hunter. Turn the damn thing on."

For once, Hunter actually did as David asked, however he had the volume turned down so low it was almost inaudible, and found a station playing something soft and classical.

"Jesus, Hunter. You're about as fun as box full of mud. Can't you at least find something from this century?"

"Deal with it, or go home."

David opened his mouth to retort, but the irritating ring of Hunter's cell phone beat him to it. David sat bolt upright, glaring at Hunter. "Don't answer it, Hunter. It'll be work again. Don't --"

Hunter shot him a dirty look and flipped his phone open. "Hunter. Yeah. Where? Aw, fuck me! Okay. Is it like the others? That's what I was afraid of. Yeah, I'm on it."

"Can't you ever *not* answer that thing? Ever heard of voice mail?" David asked. He knew without being told that Hunter had just been called in to work. He remembered those after-hour calls all too well from when he'd been alive. They were never pleasant. Nobody from the precinct ever called at this hour just to shoot the shit.

"We have a possible homicide on West Forty-seventh, just off Eleventh Avenue. Sounds like it may be our guy again. Donner said it's…messy."

"*We? Our* guy? As in yours and mine?" David huffed. "Oh no, sweet cheeks. I'm retired, remember? I'm not doing another freebie. You still haven't paid me for the Grayson case."

"If it's the same perp as the other three murders, then this asshole has killed at least four people we know of in the space of less than fourteen days, David."

"No one even knows if the cases are related, Hunter. The murder weapons were different every time. As I recall there was a two-by-four, a brick, and a ball peen hammer, and not a print left on any of them. No blood except for that of the victim. No fibers, no hair, no witnesses, no --
"

"But they've all taken place in an alley or some closed construction site, or somewhere else equally deserted, they were all vicious killings, and the victims were all young men. Nothing was stolen. The victims had no known enemies, no serious trouble with the law, no gang affiliations. For Christ's sake, David, the fact that there *wasn't* any evidence found at the scenes is a connection! I have a gut feeling about these murders. I think the same perp is responsible for all of them. The bastard gets the urge to kill, and he uses whatever's handy. This time it looks like it was a piece of PVC pipe."

"Oh man, that's not going to be pretty," David said, shaking his head.

"Come on. I need you, David," Hunter said.

David knew the words cost Hunter. Hunter was the type of man who'd rather cut out his own tongue with a rusty butter knife than ask for help from anyone, especially David. At least, that was true now that David was dead. When he'd been alive and they'd been partners, it'd been different. David missed the easy camaraderie they'd shared.

"Okay, okay, but this is the last time, Hunter. No more help until I get a little, or rather, until *you* get laid and I get to come along for the ride."

"I'll hire a prostitute if I have to, okay?"

"That's wrong on so many levels that I can't even begin to list them all. First and foremost, you're a cop, and prostitution is illegal. You won't even place a bet on the Super Bowl because of your freaking ethics, never mind pay for sex. Secondly, you don't *need* to pay for it, Hunter. You can pick up a trick at any bar in the city. You're hot, in a work-in-progress sort of way."

"Gee, thanks. That's a big compliment coming from the dead straight guy."

"Don't let it go to your head."

"I'll try."

Hunter's foot hit the gas, taking a corner on two wheels. David was unbuckled (because really, what good did a buckle do for somebody who was already dead?), and was thrown into -- and halfway out of -- the passenger side door. Only quick reflexes kept him from flying through it and doing a face plant on the street. "Whoa! What say we get there alive, Hunter? Well, one of us, anyway. What's the rush? The victim's already dead, and his body's not going anywhere."

"Maybe the ghost will still be at the scene this time." There was a hopeful note in Hunter's voice that David hated to squash.

"I wouldn't count on it, Hunter. I've told you the dead don't like to hang around their bodies, as a rule. It reminds them of dying, and everything they've left behind. Most of them hightail it out of there as soon as possible, especially the people who've died violently. They have a desperate need to put as much space as possible between themselves and the pain of their deaths. Out of sight, out of mind, you know? They go beyond the veil and never come back."

"Like you did? Oh wait…*you* never left. You're still here."

"Oh, you're a funny guy. I never crossed over, and I might remind you that I only came back after the funeral. Nobody likes to see themselves dead, Hunter. Besides, I'm only here for the sex." The last thing David wanted to admit was that *Hunter* was the true reason he'd chosen to hang around the mortal plane. He barely even admitted it to himself, but he couldn't stomach the thought of leaving Hunter alone. David would never be able to rest easy if Hunter was left behind to fend for himself. Who would watch out for him, if David didn't? A new partner? Not a chance. After David died, the chief tried getting Hunter to work with someone else. Hunter went through partners like paper napkins, used once and thrown away. He'd become so completely obnoxious, so cold and caustic, that no one could stand working with him -- except David, of course.

There was more to it than that -- a lot more. He knew his feelings for Hunter went beyond partnership and brotherly love, and while he'd been too chickenshit to face them while alive, dying had shed a completely new light on the matter. He shoved the troubling thoughts aside, not ready to deal with them, and definitely not ready to tell Hunter about them. He also knew that Hunter, as sure as shit sticks, wasn't ready to hear about it.

"I'm sorry I brought it up," Hunter grumbled.

"If you got it up more often, I'd be a much happier man."

Hunter laughed, and the sound made David smile. Hunter's laughter was a like a rare gift, seldom given freely. Even though David wasn't really hitchhiking at the moment, the connection he shared with Hunter allowed him to feel a tingle of warmth at Hunter's soft chuckle.

Both Hunter's laughter and David's warm tingling died instantly when they arrived at the murder scene.

Chapter Two

The street was awash with the flashing blue and red lights of a trio of squad cars parked at the curb. A couple of unmarked cars were parked across the way, and a coroner's van was angled at the mouth of the alley. Just beyond the coroner's van, a city sanitation truck was double-parked. In the narrow space between two crumbling brick buildings, a body lay sprawled in the harsh glare of a spotlight as one of the lab boys snapped photos and the forensics team hunted for evidence.

Hunter knew David was following him as he flashed his badge and ducked under the bright yellow crime scene tape, walking up to where the body lay. None of the uniforms paid David any mind -- they couldn't see or hear him. David was muttering under his breath, as usual. He'd always had a habit of talking to himself out loud during investigations. It used to drive Hunter nuts.

Still did.

Especially now when he couldn't even tell David to shut up without everyone around him thinking Hunter had lost what few marbles he still had rolling around inside his head. Taking a deep breath, Hunter tried to ignore David and concentrate on the victim. He could talk to David inside his head and knew David would hear him, but Hunter hated it, and refused to do it. Having conversations in his head made him feel like he was crazy, hearing voices and all that. Somehow, speaking out loud to David made having a ghost for a partner seem less...well, *nuts*.

Hunter looked down at the body lying sprawled on the blood-soaked pavement. *Male, early twenties*. At least, he *thought* the poor guy had been twenty-something -- it was hard to gage the body's age since the face was so badly beaten.

"Hey, Marty," Hunter said, standing next to a portly man in a white lab coat who held a baggie and a pair of tweezers in his hands. "What do we have?"

"Not much. One dead guy, beaten into mashed potatoes, one bloody piece of PVC pipe…that about sums it up so far, Hunter."

"Let me guess. No witnesses? No prints? No fibers? Think it's the same perp as the last three murders?"

Marty rolled his eyes. "I just started collecting the evidence, Hunter. You know I can't draw any conclusions at this stage of the game. Look, I lifted a few hairs from the dead guy's shirt, but they're the same color as *his* hair, so I wouldn't get my hopes up. There's plenty of blood, but I have no idea whether any of it belongs to someone besides the victim. Except for the blood and some gray matter, the pipe is squeaky clean. I'll take it downtown to run some more tests, but again, don't hold your breath. The body's fully clothed; I don't expect to find semen or bite marks. No witnesses were hanging around either, except for the sanitation guys who found the body when they came to empty the Dumpsters. They're over there." Marty pointed toward one of the squad cars. "All I can tell you at this point is that this guy is no longer alive. I can't even officially say he was beaten to death, although I think it's a safe bet."

"Come on, Marty. You've been a medical examiner for as many years as I've been on the force, and you're the best at what you do. What's your gut telling you?"

Marty heaved a sigh. "Okay. Off the record, my Spidey-sense tells me this will end up being the same as the other three cases you're working on, Hunter. We're not going to find jack shit helpful in the way of evidence at this scene. It's like somebody came along with a big fucking bucket of Mr. Clean and a brush, and scrubbed the scene squeaky clean."

"Yeah, that's what I was afraid of. Thanks, Marty. Let me know if the tests turn anything up, okay?" Marty's statement only confirmed what Hunter's instincts were telling him. If this scene was anything like the others, the hairs would belong to the victim, not the murderer. There would be no fingerprints, no bite marks, no footprints, no saliva, no semen, and no blood besides the victim's, and no witnesses to the crime. They were the most frustrating murders his department had ever come across. The chief had even consulted a psychic -- some dame named Peacock, of all things -- after the second murder. The mayor was breathing down the chief's neck and he was desperate, but of course, she couldn't find a damn thing either. The chief had just as swiftly booted her out of the investigation.

Like Marty said, it would be as if someone used a magic eraser to wipe clean the smallest traces of evidence from the scene.

"Sure thing, Hunter," Marty replied. He turned back to his work, squatting beside the body, and tediously picking at fibers and hairs, meticulously sealing them in small plastic baggies, and scouring the scene for anything that might prove to be useful.

"I've got something, Hunter," David said.

Hunter felt a tickle of excitement ripple up his spine as he turned to face David. "The victim?"

"What about him?" Marty asked, looking up at Hunter again.

"Oh uh…nothing. Just thinking out loud," Hunter said, smiling a crooked grin down at Marty. *Damn it.* He'd forgotten again that no one else could see or hear David. If he kept slipping up and talking to himself, the captain was going to send his ass down to psych for another evaluation. He'd been forced into going after David's death and didn't care to repeat the experience. Once was enough.

"Not the victim, sorry pal," David continued. "He's nowhere to be found. I did find a witness, though. Sort of, kind of like."

Hunter frowned. What the hell was a *sort of* witness? He jerked his chin toward the street and led David back to the car where he could ask questions without looking like a candidate for a rubber room.

As soon as he'd shut the car door, and David was seated in the passenger seat next to him, Hunter flipped open his cell phone so it would look as if he were making a call, just in case anybody was watching. "Explain," he barked.

"Jeez, check the attitude -- I'm on your side, remember? I found a woman. Nice lady, died of pneumonia about two years ago. She has some unresolved issues with her deadbeat boyfriend who drank away the money she needed to see the doctor, which is why she's still hanging around the neighborhood. Sad case, that. Anyway, she was passing the alley last night when she heard a scream. She saw two figures struggling."

"Great! She can identify the murderer!"

"Whoa, back up, pal. She's a member of the Incorporeal Club. What do you think a ghost can do for us -- pick him out of a lineup? How do you explain *that* to the district attorney? Besides, she didn't get a good look at the perp. Said he was cloaked and hooded. But she did see something else that might help us."

Hunter sighed. Of course, David was right. He couldn't very well put a ghost up on the witness stand. "So what did she see?"

"A kid. A boy, about eight years old. He was in the alley, and she told me he was watching the whole thing."

"Great. Just what I need…another ghost."

"No, she says the kid is alive."

"David, no little kid would be out here at night by himself in this neighborhood --."

"The dead have no reason to lie, Hunter. If she says there was a kid in the alley, and that he's alive, then I believe her."

"Okay. So how do we find this kid? There are only about a bajillion living in Manhattan. What does he look like? Does she know where he lives? What the hell was he doing here by himself to begin with?" Hunter asked, rubbing his face with his hand. Suddenly, he felt very, very tired.

"Yeah, okay, this is the weird part."

"More weird than a dead guy telling me that a ghost lady told him she saw a little boy at a murder scene?"

"She said he was flying."

Hunter groaned. "David, you've got to be fucking kidding me! You dragged me away from a murder investigation for this horseshit?"

"I believe her, Hunter. Well, maybe not the flying part, but the rest of it. The dead don't lie, but they *have* been known to exaggerate from time to time. Maybe the kid was sitting on top of the Dumpster, and the dark made it look like he was floating in the air to her. Anyway, she did say that she knew where to find the kid."

"Where?"

"She lived in the same building as his family. He was only five or six the last time she saw him, but she's positive that he's the son of the couple who lived in the apartment below hers. It's only a couple of blocks from here, Hunter. Over on Forty-sixth. She said the last name is Weils, but she didn't remember the kid's first name."

"Great. Dead women and flying kids. What's next…a talking unicorn shitting rainbows? Come on, David, cut me a break, will you?"

"Would it hurt to check it out, Hunter? You don't have any better leads, do you?"

Damn it. He really hated it when David was right. "I need to talk to the sanitation guys who found the body, first. Maybe they've seen something unusual." Please, God, he thought as he got out of his Dodge and made his way toward the squad cars, let them know something of value. *Please don't let my only lead be a ghost with an overactive imagination.*

* * * * *

It took only a few minutes and even fewer questions for Hunter to determine that the sanitation guys didn't know a damned thing. Just my luck, Hunter thought irritably as he dutifully scribbled the slim facts in his notebook.

The two men were dressed in dark green overalls, standard issue for the Department of Sanitation. Both were Hispanic, late twenties, and their stories were as identical as they were simple. They'd been working third shift, and had arrived at the alley about ten p.m. as usual for the scheduled pickup. They'd backed their truck up to the mouth of the alley, intending to empty the trash receptacles between the buildings. They'd discovered the body when they approached the Dumpsters. The first man, Eduardo Perez, immediately called 911 to report the crime, while the second man, Manuel Gonzalez, called their boss at the DoS. They'd returned to their truck afterward, pulled it into the street, parked, and waited for the police to arrive. They claimed not to have seen anyone in the vicinity of the alley, nor to have touched anything at the scene.

Hunter believed them. Neither man exhibited any indication of stress or guilt, aside from a slight excitement, which was most probably caused by finding the body. Both looked him directly in the eye as they gave him their statements, and when he ran their names through the squad car's onboard computer, their records came back squeaky clean. Neither had ever been in trouble with the law, aside from a few odd parking tickets. A quick call to their supervisor confirmed they'd both clocked in at nine p.m., left the DoS to begin their route shortly after, and had phoned him at approximately ten fifteen to tell him what had happened. By all accounts, Perez and Gonzalez seemed to be hardworking men who just happened to stumble across a vicious murder scene.

"No information of value there," David remarked as Hunter slid behind the wheel of his Dodge again. "I believe the DoS guys, Hunter. They didn't see anything, and they did exactly what they were supposed to do by calling it in. I'd bet my badge neither of them is the killer."

Hunter didn't remind David that David no longer had a badge to bet. Besides, he agreed. "Yeah, I know it. Shit! Why can't this ever be easy? Just once, I'd like to arrive at murder scene and find the killer hovering over the body with the murder weapon in his hand, and a full confession, neatly typed, signed, and notarized in his pocket."

David laughed. "Yeah, that'd be one for the books. Hunter, why don't we go check out the ghost lady's story? It can't hurt, and we don't have anything better to follow up on at the moment."

"All right. Let's go," Hunter said unenthusiastically. "But it's going to be a waste of time, mark my words." He started the engine, listening to the familiar wheezes and clanking as it reluctantly turned over.

"You know, I've been meaning to talk to you about this pugfugly, rattling deathtrap you drive around in," David said as Hunter put the car in gear and inched away from the curb.

"What are you talking about? This car is a classic."

"Yeah, a classic piece of shit. You need to get a new set of wheels, Hunter."

"No way. She's got some miles in her yet."

"Just enough to get her to the junkyard, I hope."

"Don't listen to him, baby," Hunter purred, patting the faded, cracked dashboard. "He doesn't know what he's talking about."

The car picked that exact moment to fart out a stream of black smoke, and give a violent shudder as the tranny kicked into gear.

"Oh yeah. She's classy, all right," David snorted.

Damn it. He really, *really* hated it when David was right.

Declining to say anything else, he headed toward the apartment building the ghost had said was the boy's address.

Chapter Three

"You do something about that boy, Emma. I don't care if you have to tie his ass to the bed at night!"

Emma Weils cringed. Bobby had begun drinking as soon as he'd come home from work and was already a twelve-pack gone, which usually only meant one thing for Emma. When Bobby Weils drank, he got angry, and when he got angry, his fists started to do the talking for him. "It won't happen again, Bobby. I swear it!"

"That's what you said the last time, isn't it? Now look what happened. He went outside, Emma. *Outside*! His hands and knees are all skinned up. It was bad enough when it was only us, finding him in the in the back of the hall closet, or in the kitchen on top of the goddamn fridge. God knows who saw him wandering around out there. People are gonna talk. What if they call in those bitches from Children and Families again? You want them to yank him away, put us in jail for abuse? I'm not doing time for that little retard."

"He *couldn't* have gotten outside. The door was locked, I swear it! It won't happen again! Please, Bob --" Emma's head rocked as Bobby backhanded her. Her hands flew to her face where she knew a bright red imprint of Bobby's hand was rising up against her pale skin.

"You're damn right it won't happen again. Do you know how embarrassing it is to have a kid like that? He won't talk. He won't look people in the eye. Just sits there rocking all day, or drawing scratches on a piece of paper like a fucking baby. He can't even stay in his bed at night! He's eight years old, Emma. He ain't gonna grow out of it like you said!"

"Please, Bobby! He can't help being this way! He --" Another brutal slap made her head reel and her eyes burn with tears. She took an inadvertent step backward, and cringed when Bobby followed.

"Shut up! I've heard enough from your mouth for one night. I should've made you get rid of him before I married you. Now you tie his ass down or I will. Got it?"

"But he's just a little boy, Bobby!"

The doorbell rang just as Bobby raised his hand, ready to swing again. He grunted in disgust and turned away, heading for the door.

Emma breathed a sigh of relief and ran for her son's bedroom. With any luck, it would be one of Bobby's friends at the door, and he'd go out to the bar with them. If he drank enough, maybe he'd come home and pass out, leaving her and Cooper alone for the night.

If God was merciful, he wouldn't come home at all.

He hadn't always been this way. She remembered a time -- it seemed like a lifetime ago now, but in reality, only six years had passed -- when Bobby had been a sweeter, kinder man. He'd opened doors for her then, brought her flowers, bought Cooper stuffed animals. When he took her to bed, he was gentle and loving. He didn't care that she had a baby out of wedlock, didn't care that her own mother had thrown her and the baby out, or that she didn't know Cooper's real daddy's name. To Bobby, Emma had been special, a lady, and Cooper was the son he never had.

That was before life took a big bite out of him, and left him with a ragged hole where his heart used to be. It happened just after they'd married. Bobby was a supervisor at the carpet factory. He'd been there forever, since he was sixteen, and had worked his way up from a stock boy. He was proud of himself, and rightly so. When the place went belly up, he lost his job. Couldn't find another, not one that paid as well. Most companies wanted their managers to have college degrees. Bobby had never even finished high school.

After that, things began to go downhill, faster and faster, until Emma felt like her life was in a free fall, plummeting toward the hard and rocky ground. Bobby got another job, but it was manual labor in a warehouse that didn't pay half what he used to earn. Emma knew Bobby thought he'd come full circle, working as a stock boy again. He tried to find the pride he'd lost in a bottle, and that was when he started to turn mean. The more he drank, the meaner he got.

When it became obvious Cooper was…different, unlike other little boys, Bobby seemed to take it as another failure on his part. At first, he tried to do right by Cooper, and she'd appreciated it. He let her take Cooper to doctors, even expensive ones not covered by state insurance. But as time went on and Cooper didn't get better, Bobby took it personally. More and more he began to shift the blame for their situation onto Cooper's thin shoulders, saying that things between him and Emma would be better if Cooper wasn't around.

God help her, sometimes after an especially vicious fight with Bobby, or after suffering an afternoon's worth of sideways stares from other mothers at the park, she thought so too.

"Emma!" Bobby's voice carried from the front door, startling her. He sounded even angrier than he'd been with her in the kitchen.

Oh, God. What now? Emma thought, panicking. Had Cooper done something wrong while he was outside last night? He was only a child, and couldn't help being the way he was. Nobody would blame him if he broke a window, or took something that didn't belong to him, would they? She didn't even know for sure he'd been outside -- she was positive the door had been locked when she went to bed because she always double-checked, and it was locked this morning when she got up. Unless Cooper unlocked it, and locked it again after returning -- which she highly doubted -- he *couldn't* have been outside the apartment. Yet there was no other explanation for his skinned hands and knees.

"Emma! Get your ass out here!"

Feeling her heart thudding in her throat, Emma crept out of Cooper's bedroom and into the living room. She stood in the doorway, her arms wrapped around herself. A man stood just inside the front door, someone she'd never seen before. He wasn't one of Bobby's friends -- she knew that at a glance. He was too well-dressed, wearing a nice button-down shirt, clean jeans, and a sports coat.

"This here is Detective Vance. Says he wants to talk to us about Cooper. I told you that kid was up to no good, didn't I? This is your fault, Emma. Told you we should've dumped him on your mother. Goddamn retard. Told you --"

"That'll be *enough*, Mr. Weils," the man said in a gravelly, stern voice. "I think perhaps you'd better wait outside while I talk to your wife."

"What? Like hell! This is my house, and I --"

"Either you leave, or I arrest you for obstruction of justice. Your choice."

"You can't fucking come in here and throw me out of my own house. You don't have a fucking warrant! I got rights! I --"

"You invited me in, and if I'm not mistaken those are fresh bruises on your wife's face. Care to explain how they got there?"

"She fell."

"Sure she did, and landed right on your fist, huh? That's a palm print on the side of her face, Mr. Weils, and she's going to have quite a shiner."

To Emma's surprise, Bobby backed down. "Fine. Do what you want." He turned to her. "I'll be at Joe's. Maybe I'll come home later. Maybe I won't," he snarled at her. The murderous look in his eye told her she'd better stick to the story he'd given the detective about falling, or she'd have more than a handprint and black eye to worry about when he came back. Grabbing his hat, he left, slamming the door behind him.

"Ma'am? I'm Detective Hunter Vance of the Midtown North Precinct. I'd like to talk to your son, if I may."

She blinked. For a second, she'd almost forgotten the detective was there. "He didn't mean anything by it. Whatever he done, he didn't mean it. Cooper is different than other kids. He can't help himself," she prattled, feeling her heart start to thump again.

"We...er...I just want to talk to him, Ma'am. That's all. He's not in trouble," Hunter said, smiling.

Emma bit her lip. "He's not in no trouble?"

"No, Ma'am."

She felt relief flood her. She believed Vance. There was something about the tall, handsome detective that made her want to trust him. Besides, he'd made Bobby leave. She felt she owed him for that favor, at least. He'd probably saved her the loss of a couple of her teeth. Bobby had really been working himself up into a state. "I'll go get Cooper."

* * * * *

The boy looked even younger than his eight years. He had tousled blond hair, huge, guileless blue eyes, and was dressed in Power Rangers pajamas. Hunter noticed new patches on the knees. Cooper clung to his mother, one skinny arm wrapped tightly around her neck. When Cooper lifted his other hand to stick his thumb into his mouth, Hunter noticed freshly scabbed, crosshatched scratches on his palm.

"Hi, Cooper. I'm Detective Vance. I wanted to ask you a couple of questions, okay?" Hunter said, keeping his tone light, smiling. He waved, but Cooper wouldn't look at him. He continued to hug his mother, head resting on her shoulder, staring at a spot somewhere behind Hunter. *Damn. Kid's shy.* "Cooper?"

"He don't talk," Emma said. Her voice dropped to a whisper, as if she were imparting a secret. "He's…the doctors said something went wrong for him when he was born -- not enough oxygen or some such. He goes to school, but they can't do much for him there. There's a private school the doctors told me about, but it's too expensive."

"He sees me, Hunter," David's awed voice whispered in his ear. "Shit, he's looking right at me! Let me try to talk to him. Tell the mother to sit him on the couch. Go talk to her in the kitchen about the bruises."

Hunter's mouth almost dropped to his knees, but he managed to recover quickly. The kid could see ghosts? That was impossible! Then again, if *he* could see David, why was it impossible for someone else to see him? Although, if the kid couldn't talk, what difference did it make if he could see David? *In any case, David is right about one thing. I* do *need to talk to her about the bruises, and the asshole she'd married to.* "Mrs. Weils, I'd like you to sit Cooper down in here while we go have a chat in the kitchen, okay?"

"Why?" Emma asked. Her voice quaked, and she shivered visibly.

Hunter promised himself that he was going to have a nice, long talk with Bobby Weils. The poor woman looked frightened half to death, and he knew damn well that the bruises on her face had been put there courtesy of her husband's temper. In fact, Hunter thought he might just forget his badge at home when he had that talk with Weils. And maybe, just maybe, he'd let Bobby Weils see what it felt like to be on the other side of a fist. "I just have a few questions, that's all. And I could really use a cup of tea, if you have some. It's been a helluva night. Okay?"

Thankfully, Emma nodded, setting Cooper on the couch. She gently peeled his arms from around her neck, kissing him on the top of the head. "Stay here, Cooper. Mama will be right back." Her frightened eyes darted to Hunter, before she led the way into the kitchen.

Chapter Four

Well, I'll be good goddamned, David thought, looking into Cooper's wide blue eyes. He took a step to the left, then another to the right, and watched Cooper's eyes follow him. *He can really see me. The only other living person I've met who can do that is Hunter. I always figured it was because we were friends, and he has empathic abilities. Maybe the kid is an empath too. A psychic. Amazing.* "Hi, Cooper," he said, raising a hand and waggling his fingers at him. "You can see me, huh?"

Cooper nodded, just the tiniest bit of movement, but there was comprehension in his eyes.

"Can you talk, Coop?"

Again, Cooper responded with a minute nod. *"Yes."*

David heard Cooper answer him, but the child's lips never moved. *Holy crap. The kid is telepathic. Cool!* Since he'd died, David had come to accept things he'd have scoffed at while alive. Things like ghosts, for example -- or flying, telepathic kids. "I'm Detective Brown. Would you answer a few questions for me, Cooper?"

"Okay."

"Do you talk to anyone else like this?"

"No. I try, but Mama doesn't hear me."

"I'm sure she wants to, big guy. She loves you a bunch, you know."

"I know. I love her too. Will you tell her for me?"

David felt a distinct pang in the vicinity of his heart, and figured he was picking up an echo of emotion from Cooper. "She knows, kid. She knows. No one can hear me, either, except for Hunter. He's the other policeman."

"Are you dead?"

"Yeah, Cooper. I am." *Smart kid. And not the least bit afraid of me. Remarkable.* "How did you know?"

Cooper stuck his thumb in his mouth, sucking noisily. *"I see other people like you sometimes, but I don't talk to them, 'cause they're strangers and Mama says never to go with strangers. Does it hurt to be dead?"*

"Naw. I'm good." *Hunter can't see other ghosts. Only me, but this kid can. He's freaking incredible.* His curiosity about Cooper inched up another notch.

"I think Bobby wants to make me dead. He's not my real daddy, and he doesn't like me much. I don't like him, either. He hits Mama sometimes. Me, too, when I'm bad. Sometimes I can't help being bad, though."

David paused. If he didn't know better, he'd swear that was anger he felt roiling up in his gut. It was impossible, though. Cooper didn't look angry, therefore David couldn't be hitchhiking on his emotions. *Hunter must be getting pissed off in the kitchen. Probably because of the mother's bruises.* He shook it off. "Well, I think Detective Hunter will make sure that doesn't happen anymore, Coop. Say, I heard that you went out last night all by yourself," David said, changing the subject, trying to sound casual, as if it were no big deal that an eight-year-old went outside alone at night in this part of the city. He paused again when Cooper blanched a pale white. "It's okay, Cooper. Nobody's angry with you."

"Bobby is. I heard him yelling at Mama. He hit her too. I can't help being bad sometimes," he repeated.

"Well, Bobby's not here, and I don't think you were being bad, Cooper." And Bobby won't be coming back, if I have anything to say about it, David silently added. "So…did you? Go out last night?"

Cooper paused, as if he were trying to decide whether to tell David the truth or not, then gave another tiny nod. *"I went flying."*

There it was. Unbelievably, Cooper was verifying what the ghost lady had told David. How could it be possible, though? "You can fly? That's so cool!"

"Only when I'm asleep. Nobody can see me except for people like you, but I see them. Nobody yells at me or calls me names when I'm sleeping, either. I fly way up high, and in between the buildings. It's fun. But I wish I could be in my bed when I wake up. That's what makes Bobby so mad. 'Cause I'm never in my bed in the morning. But last night…"

Cooper's voice faded, and his thumb-sucking intensified. Small, wet sounds filled the silence between them. David saw a shiver ripple across Cooper's thin shoulders.

"What about last night, Coop?" David urged gently. He didn't want to push the kid too hard, but he needed to know what Cooper had seen.

"The Bad Man saw me last night. I was so scared!" Cooper cried in David's head. He began to shake, rocking back and forth on the sofa.

"I'm sorry you were scared, Cooper, but you're home now, and safe. I'm here, and Detective Hunter is in the kitchen with your mom, remember? No one can hurt you. We won't let them." *Damn, this is getting weirder by the minute! The kid can fly in his dreams? How? It must be some sort of astral projection. And some breather is out there who can see kids sleep-*

flying? No, that part doesn't make a lick of sense. He must mean the dead neighbor, David decided. *He said people like me can see him. The dead can see the living, so they must also see Cooper when he dreams.*

Cooper spoke in David's head again. *"He was a bad man. Real bad. He was by the big garbage can, and was hitting another man with a white pipe. I think he made the other man dead."*

Oh shit. The killer *was the one who saw Cooper? That's impossible!* Then again, Cooper and Hunter could *both* see David. If he'd found two true psychics in the same city, was it so far out of the realm of impossibility that there would be a third? One who could see a little boy's astral projection? "How do you know that he saw you?" David asked, afraid of the answer.

"I was watching him, and he looked right back at me, and I was really scared. I think he wanted to make me dead too."

"Well, you're safe now," David repeated, trying to calm Cooper down. The kid looked like he was going to start bawling at any minute, and David still had to get more information out of him. *Maybe Cooper just* thought *the guy saw him.* Yeah, that must be it, David thought, feeling relieved at what seemed a likely explanation.

"He scared me so bad that I fell down," Cooper said, holding out a pudgy hand toward David. David could see the red scabbing of scrapes across Cooper's palm. *"I never fell down in my dreams before. Then he came after me. I think he was going to hit me with the pipe, too, like he did the other man, but I woke up before he could."*

David felt his short-lived relief drain away, replaced by a heavy sense of foreboding. The man went after Cooper? That implied he *had* seen Cooper, and it wasn't Cooper's imagination after all. That wasn't good. Not good at all.

He looked at Cooper's raw, angry palms, and suddenly saw the patches on the knees of his pajamas. "Those are awesome pj's, Coop. Wish I had a pair like that. Were you wearing them last night when you went flying?"

"Uh huh. They're my favorites. Mama fixed them this morning."

Oh, man. How the hell does a kid get his hands scraped up like that, and rip open the knees of his pajamas in his sleep? He paused for a moment, looking around. There was threadbare, beige carpeting in the living room, and he was willing to bet that the same construction grade rugs were throughout the house. There was probably linoleum in the kitchen and bathroom, nothing that might account for the damage David was seeing. The kid didn't scrape his palms and rip his pajamas on carpeting and linoleum. He needed concrete for that.

David looked back at Cooper, filing his thoughts away for the moment. "Coop, you're a big boy, right?" he asked, and got a nod from Cooper in return. "Can I ask you a question without you getting really scared on me?"

Cooper nodded again, a little more hesitantly than the first. He sucked harder on his thumb.

"Can you tell me what the bad man looked like? If you tell me, then I can catch him and put him in jail so he can't hurt anybody else."

"He was really ugly. Scary. He had funny black marks all over his face."

"Funny marks? You mean tattoos?"

"No. Bobby has those on his arms. The Bad Man's were ugly. I think maybe he got hurt."

"Could they have been scars or burns?"

A thin shoulder lifted. *"Maybe. I guess so."*

"Was he tall? Fat? Thin? Did he have a beard or a mustache?"

"Don't remember. He was bigger than the other man. The one he was hitting."

The victim had been a man of medium height and build. Good. That gave David a better idea of the man they were looking for. Larger than average, burned or scarred face…that should narrow it down to only a thousand or so men in the city, he thought dryly.

"Okay. Thanks, Cooper. You've been a big help to me," David said. The kid had obviously had enough. He was rocking faster, and sucking that thumb a mile a minute. "Want to go to your mom?"

A nod, then Cooper slipped off the couch, hurrying toward the kitchen. David followed behind him.

He found Hunter sitting at a battered Formica table, sipping tea from a crackled Yankees mug. Emma Weils sat across from him, looking scared out of her wits. The bruises on her face were turning a dark, angry purple, and her lip and eye were swelling. "You're not going to believe this," he told Hunter, "but the kid is telepathic. He could talk to me in my head. I got a description of the killer, but we have to have a conversation about this. I think the kid may be in danger."

"Mrs. Weils," Hunter said, as if he hadn't heard David. "I really think you should go to a shelter tonight. Nobody has the right to hit you. *Ever*."

"No, no shelter. He'd only find us and bring us back. That's what happened before," Mrs. Weils said softly, shaking her head. "It'll be worse then." She held out her arms, and Cooper climbed into them, cuddling close.

"We wouldn't let that happen this time, Emma."

"I'll…I'll think about it, okay?" Mrs. Weils said, touching the business card that sat on the table next to her untouched cup of tea. Hunter had written his cell phone number on the back.

David looked into Hunter's eyes. "It's not his father that I'm worried about, Hunter. It's the killer. Cooper said the killer *saw* him." He watched a muscle twitch in Hunter's jaw as he stood up.

"If you change your mind, you have my number," Hunter said. "Remember, call any time, day or night, okay?"

Mrs. Weils nodded, but David doubted that she would. He'd seen the same look in other women's eyes far too many times as a cop when he'd been alive. It was fear, the kind that came at the hands of an abusive spouse. He wondered how long it would be before Bobby Weils lost control and Mrs. Weils joined the ranks of the Incorporeal Club.

"Oh yeah…" Hunter said, as if he'd suddenly remembered something. "Don't open the door for anyone you don't know, and don't let Cooper outside. There was a murder nearby last night, and the killer hasn't been apprehended yet. Okay?"

"Okay. I'll watch him, make sure he doesn't leave the house," Emma said softly, hugging Cooper closer to her breast.

"Hunter?" David said, before Hunter could leave the room. "Tell her that he loves her."

Hunter shot him a puzzled, *are-you-crazy* look.

"Just do it, okay? I'll explain later," David said.

"Emma?" Hunter said after heaving a sigh. "Cooper loves you."

Her eyes blinked up at him, surprised, then down at her son, misting. "I know he does. He can't talk and tell me so, but I know it."

"Thank you, Mr. Ghost," Cooper's voice sang in David's head.

"No problem, kid. I'll come see you again, and remember…don't be afraid, Cooper. Everything's going to be all right," David said, fervently hoping that he wasn't lying to him. "But promise me that you won't go flying until I say it's safe. Promise me, Cooper."

"I promise."

David prayed that the kid would be true to his word. If the kid could scrape his hands and knees while dreaming, then it might be possible for the murderer to hurt Cooper if he got his hands on the boy, even in a dream.

All the more reason they needed to find the killer, and find him fast.

* * * * *

"What the hell happened in there?" Hunter asked the moment they left the apartment.

"You can arrest Weils for abusing his wife, you know. Technically, you're required to by the state."

"I know it, but she won't press charges, and he'll be released in a day or so. Then what happens? He comes back, and gives her a double dose."

"Do you suppose 'Joe's' is that seedy little dive over on Forty-ninth? I think we should pay Mr. Weils a visit. Maybe you can at least put the fear of God into him. The fucker is one foul bastard."

"Yeah, it could be the same place. Personally, I'd like his face to get up close and personal with my knuckles. But first, I want to know what the kid said," Hunter pressed.

David floated down the stairs, not bothering to simulate walking. "This whole case is getting more bizarre by the minute, Hunter. The kid? First of all, he's psychic, like you, except stronger. He can see and hear me, no doubt about it. He's also telepathic. I could hear him speaking in my head as clearly as you can hear me now. Smart as a whip too. He told me he can fly in his dreams and that last night he met up with our killer. Worse, he said the killer could see him."

"In his dreams? Come on, David. The kid had a nightmare, that's all. Nobody can fly for real, in their dreams or not, unless they're in a plane."

"At first that's what I thought too, but he knew about the PVC pipe, and what the victim looked like, what the alley was like. The dead neighbor lady saw him too. How do you explain all that? Did you notice that Cooper's hands were scraped up, and his pajamas were patched at the knee? He told me that he'd fallen in his dream when the killer looked at him."

"That's impossible!"

"Then how do you explain what the kid knows?"

"I can't even explain how a child can speak to you in your head. For that matter, I can't explain how *I'm* talking to a corpse."

"Hey! I'm not a corpse. *Corpse* implies having a *body*, which in case you haven't noticed, I'm lacking."

"Trust me. I've noticed. Maybe Cooper was actually *there*, at the scene. Have you thought of that? Hell, maybe Bobby Weils is the murderer, and took Cooper along for a father/son bashing spree."

"You met Weils. Does he seem like the type that could cover his tracks so perfectly that there wasn't a single scrap of evidence at the scene?"

Hunter grunted. "He doesn't seem bright enough to tie his own shoelaces without a schematic."

"Well, there you go. I doubt seriously that Cooper was anywhere near that murder scene…at least, not in the flesh." David stopped walking, turning to face Hunter. "Look. If there's one thing you should have learned by now, it's that that there's more to our world than can be explained by science. Take me, for example. I'm dead and yet I'm still here, and you can see and hear me. Is it really any more impossible that Cooper might be telepathic? Or that reality intrudes into his dreams?"

Hunter nodded hesitantly. "Yeah, okay. I don't want to, but I'll give you that much."

"Good. This is what I think. You remember my explanation of how I can manipulate space? How I can travel from here to there in a blink?"

"Yeah, that whole 'space is like a blanket' crap."

"It's not crap," David retorted, affronted. "It's a perfectly good analogy. Anyway, I think Cooper can do me one better. I think he can manipulate *reality*, Hunter. I think that when Cooper dreams he's flying, he really is...or at least some *form* of him is flying."

"Like an out-of-body experience?" Hunter asked, quirking an eyebrow.

David wanted to smack the cynical look off his face. *You'd think a guy who had a ghost as a best friend would be more open to new ideas.* "Yes, like astral projection, but more so...more *real*. He flew last night and he was injured in his 'dream.' Those injuries showed up on his hands and knees this morning. Plus, he told me that when he wakes up, he's never in his bed. That implies that his corporeal body is moving during his dreams."

"Do you honestly think the kid physically flies around the city at night like some eight-year-old Superman? That's a stretch, David, even for you."

"No, but I do think that he can manipulate reality in a way that allows his physical-self to link so closely with his dream-self that the two are virtually inseparable. If he moves in his dream, his physical body does too, only not as far -- maybe only from his bed to the living room, or the kitchen, but it still moves. If he's hurt in his dream, he's hurt in real life. That's scary stuff, Hunter."

"No shit. So that could be why his mother finds him in odd places in the morning. She said she's found him in the closet, under the sink, and once on top of the fridge."

"Yeah. It must be a by-product of the link between his dreams and reality. It's strong enough to move his body around the house. I'm more surprised that Mrs. Weils has never caught him at it."

"Fuck. You're making me dizzy with this New Age shit."

"Yeah? Well fasten your seat belt, Hunter, because this spin cycle is about to go into overdrive. You've missed the most important detail in Cooper's story."

"Which would be…?"

"That the killer saw him. *Saw* him, Hunter."

Hunter frowned, looked puzzled. "So? I can see *you*."

David sighed. Seriously, sometimes Hunter could be as thick as a brick. "Yeah, except Cooper isn't a ghost, but he isn't flesh and blood when he flies, either. If he were, surely somebody in this city would've spotted an eight-year-old in Power Ranger pajamas flying around town. Cooper's form is basically incorporeal like mine. The living don't ordinarily see ghosts. *You* can see me because you're empathic, and because we were so close during my life. Cooper sees me because of his unique psychic abilities."

"Are you saying that…no, that's ridiculous!"

"But I think it's true. Our killer may be another psychic, Hunter."

"Come on, David!"

"Wait, it gets better. There's an alternate explanation."

Hunter swiped a hand across his face, and then shoved his fingers through his hair, a sign David knew meant he was nearing information overload. He pressed on, before Hunter could cut him off. "The killer *could* be a ghost, Hunter."

"What? Oh no…now I know for sure that you're crazy!"

"Think about it! It fits, Hunter. It explains everything -- why there are never any witnesses to the crime, never any evidence left at the scene, and why he was able to see Cooper. Cooper told me that he sees other ghosts when he flies, and that they see him. I think Cooper didn't realize the killer was a ghost, and Cooper was so surprised when the killer went after him, that he fell."

"Okay, then answer me this, Sherlock: If the killer is a ghost, then how did he use a PVC pipe to kill someone? You said that you can't touch anything -- hence the entire "hitchhiking" thing you came up with, remember?"

"That's the one part I can't figure out." Hunter had a point. David *didn't* know how a ghost could manage to cross the barrier between life and death far enough to manipulate objects, or how a ghost could become angry enough to murder someone, for that matter. "Unless," David said, thinking out loud, "he was hitchhiking on the emotions of the victims!"

"Say again?"

"What do we know about the victims, Hunter? Were they having problems? At work, at home, with a lover? Has anyone investigated their emotional state prior to their deaths?"

Hunter fell silent for a moment. David could almost see him flipping through the case files in his mind. "The first, Kenneth Johnson, was in the middle of a nasty divorce. His wife was ruled out as a suspect because she had an alibi. The second, Martin Wilthrop, had a history of mental illness, including being prone to violent outbursts. The third, Stan Flint, was an accountant. He was being investigated for embezzling funds, and although no charges were pending at the time of his death, there was a report of him having a shout-down with his boss on the night he was murdered. His boss had an alibi too. We don't know anything yet about the man who was found tonight, though."

"See? It all fits! If our psycho-ghost wanted to kill, all he had to do was find someone who was really angry and feed off their emotional juices."

"Like some kind of psychic vampire? Do you realize how crazy that sounds?"

"Crazier than me leeching off your orgasms?"

"Point taken," Hunter grumbled. "It still doesn't explain how he could manipulate physical objects."

David wasn't about to let go of this theory so easily. He had a hunch about it that went bone-deep. "Being dead doesn't come with a handbook, you know. I didn't *know* about hitchhiking on emotions…I figured it out. What if it's possible for a ghost to *learn* to touch stuff? What if the killer mastered the art?"

To prove his point, David laid his hand on Hunter's arm. It passed right through him. David swore softly and tried again, with the same results. "Then again, maybe he's just a psychic -- albeit a psychotic one -- who's a genius at covering his tracks."

"Shit. Flying kids, vampire ghosts, psychic serial killers…come on. My mind can't handle this shit now. We're going to Joe's and have a talk with Bobby Weils, and after I've convinced him that beating up his wife can be hazardous to his health, I'm going to get shitfaced," Hunter said. "Maybe *then* this crap will make sense to me."

David followed Hunter to the car, his mind in a whirl. He didn't want to let go of the idea that the killer might be a ghost. It somehow rang true for him, and the possibility fascinated him.

Was it feasible? If it were, could *David* actually learn to touch things? If so, could he learn to *feel* things again without having to hitchhike on Hunter's emotions?

Watching Hunter slide behind the wheel, David came to a decision. He didn't know if any of it was possible, but he was going to find out.

Chapter Five

Joe's was indeed a seedy hole-in-the-wall, the kind of bar that was frequented by hard-drinking men with very little self-control and very big chips on their shoulders. The only glasses that lined the shelves behind the bar were shot glasses, rock glasses, and beer mugs. There were no wineglasses in evidence; no brandy snifters or liqueur glasses. It was the kind of place that had only three items on its menu -- Bud and Miller on tap, and hard booze; a place where manhood was measured in liquid ounces.

It was dark inside, and warm. Ceiling fans turned lazily, doing nothing to dispel the odor of cheap booze and perspiration that clung to the yellowed walls and ceiling. There were only two people in the place -- the bartender, an older, heavyset man with a balding pate and a nose shot through with red veins, and one customer.

Hunter flashed his badge, convincing the bartender to suddenly find something important to do in the back room. The man disappeared, moving faster than Hunter would have thought he could.

Bobby Weils sat on a stool at the far corner of the bar, hunched over his beer. An empty shot glass rested on the counter next to the brew. Hunter could only imagine how many the man had sucked down in the short amount of time he'd been gone. Weils' head bobbed over the glass, and when he tipped it to his lips, liquid dribbled sloppily from his lip. From the looks of him and the half-empty bottle of Jack D on the bar, beer had been chasing whiskey since he'd left his house earlier that night.

"Hey, Bobby," Hunter said, tapping him on the shoulder. Weils turned his head, but didn't answer. He blinked bleary eyes at Hunter. "We're finished at your house. Oh yeah…and so are you."

Hunter caught a flash of anger fighting the liquor-induced fuzz in Weils' eyes. "Yeah? That what my wife told you? That she don't want me there no more? Fuck her. It's *my* house. I get home, I'll teach that bitch whose boss."

Hunter resisted the urge to fan his hand in front of his nose. Weils' breath was enough to drop a rhino at twenty paces. "No, you're not. You won't be going anywhere near your wife or Cooper again."

"What are you gonna do? Fuckin' arrest me for going to my own house? That bitch swear out a warrant for me again or something? Well, fuck her!" Weils slurred, slamming his beer down onto the bar. He didn't seem to notice the amber liquid that sloshed over the rim. "It's her word against mine. It's my house! He was supposed to get better. She promised. Did she tell you that? No, I guess not, huh? She promised he'd get better. I took him to the doctors, like she asked, but he never changed. Took me for a ride, that's what she did, her and him both. Well, her and her retard kid can go sleep in the gutter for all I care."

Hunter fought back a smile. Weils was working himself into a dangerous mood, and was drunk enough to take it to the next level -- which was exactly what Hunter was hoping would happen. He leaned in closer, getting in Bobby's personal space even though Bobby smelled like a sewer. "You're not going *anywhere*. You like beating on women, do you? Makes you feel like a man? I'll bet you're a homo, and you hit on your wife because you can't get it up with her. That sound about right, Bobby?"

"You fucking asshole! I'm no fucking queer!" Weils bellowed, sliding off the stool. He teetered for a minute, then found his balance and swung his fist wildly, nicking Hunter on the jaw.

Hunter jerked his head to the side, biting back a smile. *Oh, yeah. Playing the gay card - works every fucking time with these bozos. Never mind that I just accused Weils of beating his wife -- I did far worse than that. I insulted his manhood. Stupid bastard.* "Shit, you even hit like a girl."

Weils roared, and grabbed the bottle of Jack by the neck and smashed the body against the bar. He jabbed the jagged glass at Hunter's face. He missed by a mile, but it was the move Hunter had been waiting for.

"Know what?" he asked, grabbing Weils' wrists. In one smooth movement, he cracked Weils' wrist against the bar, making him drop the bottleneck, then twisted Weils around, bending him over the bar. Slapping the metal cuffs he pulled from his pocket on Weils' wrists, Hunter leaned in and growled, "That, you jackass, was assault with a deadly weapon, and on a police officer to boot. That's heavy shit, son. You're under arrest. Oh yeah…and I'm one of those of fucking queers, you sorry son of a bitch."

Holding Weils down with one hand -- an easy feat since Weils was three sheets to the wind and barely able to stand on his own -- Hunter dug out his phone, flipped it open, and called the precinct for a squad car.

David stood next to him, applauding. "Nice work, Hunter. Couldn't have done it better myself. Although I must say that it would have been a helluva lot more satisfying to see you deck him. Come on…at least just bruise him a little."

Hunter ignored David, shuffling Weils over to the wall, letting him slide heavily down to the floor. "Sit. Don't move. Don't make me have to shoot you."

"Ooh, now that would be infinitely *more* than satisfying. *That* would make me come in my pants," David said.

"You perv," Hunter grinned.

"Not a fuckin' perv," Weils moaned.

"Shut up," Hunter said to Weils. "I wasn't talking to you."

Uniforms arrived and took Weils away with orders from Hunter to read him his rights and book him for assault on a police officer, the weapons charge, spousal abuse, and anything else they could come up with. Out of the slew of charges, something was bound to stick and put the bastard away for a quite a while, at least long enough for Emma Weils to file for divorce and start over somewhere else.

Hunter walked outside and made a second call, this time to Emma Weils. He explained what had happened, that Weils was going to jail for a long time, and reminded her to keep a close eye on Cooper, promising to check in on them the next day.

Her gratitude was almost embarrassing. He felt his cheeks pink as he hung up.

"Okay. Score one for the good guys. One bad guy down, one killer still to go. What do you want to do now?" David asked. "Still want to get drunk?"

"Oh *hell*, yeah. I need it after today's weird-fest," Hunter replied, slipping behind the wheel of his car. "I can go to the precinct and write up the paperwork on Weils tomorrow." He glanced out the window at Joe's, trying to decide whether to get back out and park his ass on the nearest barstool or go somewhere else.

"Don't even *think* about it, Hunter. I'm not going back into that rattrap. I wouldn't let my cockroaches drink out of the glasses in that cesspool," David said. "Feathers isn't too far from here. That's where you were headed originally. Let's go there."

Hunter couldn't even bring himself to argue. He started the car, shifted it into gear, and headed toward the club.

* * * * *

After the stink and dimly lit shabbiness of Joe's, the lights and music of Feathers seemed almost too bright, too loud.

Hunter squinted against the glare, threading his way through the crowd to the long, chrome bar. His mind was buzzing, overloaded with new ideas, most of which he desperately wanted to dismiss out-of-hand as claptrap. Telepathic kids who flew in their dreams? Psycho ghosts who could reach from beyond the grave to kill the living? It was too bizarre, too outrageous to be believable, and yet the fact that his "partner" was a ghost made the fantastical all too damn possible.

David's theory that the perp might be alive and a psychic had too many holes in it to suit Hunter. It didn't explain why there was never any evidence found at the murder scenes, not even of the microscopic variety, or any witnesses -- except for a ghost, and a flying, eight-year-old mute boy.

His other idea, the one Hunter wanted to discount the most, had an unmistakable ring of truth to it no matter what Hunter insisted to the contrary. He couldn't shake the feeling that David was on to something. David's hypothesis that the killer was dead, no matter how crazy, made sense. If true, the theory presented an even bigger problem: how did he go about arresting a fucking ghost?

He needed a drink, probably more than one, to quiet the tumult in his mind, and slid onto the first available barstool. "Bourbon on the rocks," he said once he had the bartender's attention. "Heavy on the bourbon, light on the rocks."

"You got it," the bartender answered with a slow, sultry smile.

Hunter observed the bartender expertly pour the drink; there was long practice in the bartender's sure and purposeful movements. Tall, with dark, spiky hair, the man had a nice smooth chest under his sleeveless, black leather vest, wickedly sculpted biceps, and a stomach that Hunter could've used to scrub his laundry. Nice to watch, he thought, accepting his drink, grateful for the minute or two of distraction from his worries.

"Talk to him," David's voice whispered in Hunter's ear. "Go for it."

Aw, shit. He'd forgotten that David was there. He shook his head minutely, taking a long swallow of bourbon that burned like napalm on the way down.

"Come on, Hunter. You need a break and so do I. Look…he's into you. He's staring at you. Smile, for God's sake!"

Against his better judgment, Hunter looked up at the hot bartender and smiled.

"Oh man. You've been out of circulation for too long. Put a little more *friendly* and a lot less *serial killer* into that smile, will ya?" David said. "You look like a rabid dog baring its teeth."

Hunter dropped both his eyes and his smile and sipped at his drink, feeling the knot that had formed between his shoulders tighten. It was at times like this when he really wished David was corporeal, just so Hunter could deck him.

"I don't remember seeing you in here before." A tanned hand with long, expressive fingers swept a cloth over the bar in front of Hunter, cleaning a nonexistent spot on the gleaming surface. Looking up, Hunter found the bartender's warm brown eyes watching him. "I'm Justin."

"Been here a couple of times," Hunter mumbled, then repeated it, raising his voice so Justin could hear him over the din in the club.

"Your name, idiot! Tell him your name," David hissed into his ear. "And smile!"

"Oh...uh, I'm Hunter." *Jesus.* He felt like a schoolboy at his first mixer. It was a sorry state of affairs when a man had to take dating advice from a ghost, especially when, as Hunter recalled, the ghost was straight, hadn't managed to get very much action while he was alive, and could hardly be considered an expert on the gay dating scene.

"Hey, Hunter. Cool name. Sexy," Justin smiled. He'd stopped cleaning and had rested his hands on either side of Hunter's.

Nice hands. Long, elegant fingers. Pianist hands. Not like his own, scarred and calloused, nails chewed down to the quick. *Bet they'd be able to massage some of the tension out of my neck...and other body parts.* He felt his body stir at the prospect.

"Ask him out!" David hissed in his ear.

"Uh, when do you get off?" Hunter asked before he could stop himself, and immediately winced, feeling his face heat up at his own, wholly unintentional, double entendre.

Justin chuckled, his full lips quirking up in a sexy smile. "That depends on how fast we can get to your place after my shift here ends at two."

"Oh, I *like* him. A man after my own heart," David said, laughing. "Say *yes*, Hunter."

Hunter tossed back his bourbon, and shook his head. "Not possible...my place is on the other side of town." There was no way in cold hell was he bringing a stranger home with him to his private, inner sanctum, no matter *what* David said to the contrary. He was a cop, damn it, and knew better than that. He ignored the steady stream of obscenities as David raked him over the coals for not jumping at the chance to take Justin home for the night.

"That's okay. I know of a hotel right around the corner that's cheap and has hourly rates," Justin said. His fingers moved, lightly stroking over Hunter's hand. "Or, we have a black room here. It's downstairs."

"I think I'll opt for the hotel," Hunter said. The last thing he needed was to get mauled in the dark by horny men in the bar's downstairs sex room, or God forbid, get caught up in a raid.

Justin's touch, feather-soft and all too brief, nevertheless caused Hunter's groin to tighten and his cock to stiffen. David was right. He really *did* need to get laid. "Cool," he said, ignoring David's whoop of victory.

In truth, Hunter felt like crowing a little himself. It had been so long since he'd last picked up a guy that it felt kind of good to know that he still had it. Now he only hoped his skills between the sheets hadn't grown rusty. *Get a grip. How bad could it be?* It's like riding a bike, he told himself, trying hard not to remember how long it had been since he'd taken that particular bike out for a spin. He could only hope the tires hadn't gone flat and the chain wasn't broken. Forcing himself to smile at Justin, he ordered another drink and hoped for the best.

Chapter Six

The Palace Motel had absolutely *nothing* palatial about it, aside from a startling resemblance to the dungeons that might have existed in the lowest levels of a medieval castle. The exterior was a tired, dingy gray, in dire need of a fresh coat of paint -- not counting the colorful graffiti that covered most of it -- and the front office was barely larger than a closet. A man sat at a counter inside the front door protected by a steel grate cage, watching a tiny, portable television set. Taped to the cage were hand-printed notices that read NOT RESPONSIBLE FOR THEFT and CASH ONLY. Money for the room rental had to be slipped to him through a small slot at the bottom of the grate. A brass key, blackened with age and attached to a cracked plastic rectangle printed with the numbers205, was slid back the same way.

The stairway stank of urine; each step was littered with old fast food containers, empty beer bottles, and sprinkled with a confetti of stubbed out cigarettes, joints, used poppers, and condoms. Phone numbers and obscene, barely legible phrases and stick figures were scrawled on the wall in a variety of mediums, including pencil, pen, permanent marker, and something that looked suspiciously to Hunter like blood. His skin crawled, and he was seriously tempted to turn tail and put as much distance between himself and the hotel as possible. Only the pleading, hound dog look on David's face, and the way Justin's ass filled out the back of his pants kept him moving up the stairs.

He was instantly sorry the moment he entered the room -- it was even worse than the stairwell.

Room 205 completely and utterly reeked. The disinfectant used by housekeeping didn't mask the stench of mold, body odor, weed, piss, and sex that permeated the room – it only added to it. Even David wrinkled his nose upon entering, which said something about the power of the odor. It *had* to be bad if it offended a dead guy.

Besides the stink, there was nothing noteworthy about the room. It was completely bare except for a bed made over with a thin blanket (Hunter instantly made up his mind that there was no way his naked skin was going near it), a nightstand, and one slat-backed chair that didn't match the other two pieces of furniture. No dresser, no television, no phone. The walls were a yellowed off-white that darkened to brown near the ceiling from old cigarette smoke, without a single thing to decorate them aside from the abstract patterns made by the cracking, peeling paint. It was illegal to smoke in hotel rooms in New York City anymore, but evidently, the establishment of the Palace Hotel hadn't gotten the memo.

Hunter doubted that he'd find anything in the tiny bathroom except for perhaps a threadbare towel and a miniature bar of paper-wrapped soap. Then again, he supposed the men who rented rooms at the Palace didn't really need amenities…well, nothing except for the small, complimentary tube of lube and foil-wrapped condom sitting on the scarred nightstand.

Justin, as it turned out, was not a man who wasted time on pleasantries like conversation or foreplay. No sooner had he shooed Hunter into the room and locked the door behind them than he began to strip. "Come on, get the lead out," he said, shimmying out of his pants, "we've only got the room for an hour."

David took a seat on the chair, facing the bed. Hunter locked eyes with him, and felt the minute jolt sizzling between his ears signaling the completion of the psychic connection that would enable David to hitchhike on Hunter's emotions. Hunter could barely keep from rolling his eyes as David allowed the illusion of clothing to melt away from his body, stretched his legs out in front of him and got ready to watch the show. His cock was already stirring, mirroring what Hunter felt at Justin's straightforward attitude. He turned away from David, refusing to look at him anymore, and focused on Justin.

The sleek skin Justin exposed as he stood in front of Hunter in nothing but a skimpy pair of black bikini briefs, his thick cock clearly outlined under the thin material, was enough to nearly make Hunter forget David was in the room. Justin was tall, long through the waist, and narrow at the hips. Every inch of him was perfectly sculpted; he either had fantastic genes or spent an inordinate amount of time in the gym. There wasn't an inch of fat to spare anywhere on his frame. His left nipple was pierced by a shiny silver ring.

When Justin shed his underwear, his cock sprang up hard and ready, and he closed his fingers around his thick shaft. Hunter was mesmerized by the neatly trimmed triangle of hair pointing toward Justin's prick like an arrow. It'd been a good, long while since Hunter was this close to a naked man who wasn't dead, particularly one who looked as good as Justin, and all he could do was stare.

David's reproachful voice penetrated his mind. "Hunter, you need to get a move on or Justin's going to party without you. Strip down! He's bare-assed, and you haven't even taken your shirt off yet. Has it been so long since you last got laid that you don't remember you need to be naked to have sex?"

"Shut up!" Hunter hissed in his mind, but he shrugged out of his shirt and went work on his pants, moving faster than before. *"I'm trying to forget you're here, David!"*

David pointed toward Justin, whose head was down, watching his hand slide along his shaft as he stroked himself. "Yeah? Well, if you don't hurry up, Justin is going to forget that *you're* here and whack off."

"It's bad enough that you have to be here, but do you have to keep flapping your gums too?" Hunter yelled at David, albeit in his head. He stepped out of his pants and underwear, feeling a little self-conscious as David's eyes crawled over him, particularly when they stopped and stared at the juncture between Hunter's legs. To Hunter's dismay, his cock thickened, his body responding as much to the hungry look in David's eyes as to the show Justin was putting on. His cheeks heated as a disturbing through danced through his head. *I wish David was still alive.*

David realized that he knew Hunter's body almost as well as he'd known his own when he'd had one.

Without looking, David knew Hunter had a mole on the inside of his powerful left thigh; knew he had a small scar on his forehead near the hairline, and remembered it'd come from a piece of flying glass during one of the busts they'd made together. There were two, perfect dimples on his backside, one atop each of his ass cheeks, and a tattoo at the nape of Hunter's neck of the black half of the *taijitu* symbol.

He remembered Hunter had it done shortly after David died, and David knew it represented the missing half of Hunter's yin and yang -- *him*, even though Hunter had never told him as much. It was Hunter's touching private tribute to the loss of their partnership. David thought it was one of the sweetest things Hunter had ever done, and totally out of character, which only told David how highly Hunter had thought of him.

They'd butted heads at nearly every turn during the first year they'd been assigned together on the vice squad, back when Hunter had first been promoted to detective, the smell of a beat cop still clinging to his skin. David was a veteran whose partner had retired when a bullet left him with a limp and a disability check.

David remembered Hunter as being so full of energy, so brimming with the save-the-world mentality common to new detectives that he would charge into a bust like the fucking cavalry, rarely using his head. David had needed to drag him back from the edge of catastrophe time and time again. Eventually, he and Hunter had finally smoothed out the edges of their prickly relationship until it was virtually seamless. They'd developed a deep understanding of each other over the next decade, becoming closer than brothers. David grew to know what Hunter was thinking almost before Hunter did, and vice versa.

Right now, he knew Hunter was thinking he'd like to lick Justin all over, starting at the graceful arch of Justin's feet and working his way up to those full, pouty lips, with a long, leisurely stop at the area between Justin's thighs and belly button. David's cock bobbed its head in agreement. "Go for it, Hunter," he said, fisting himself.

"Shut up," Hunter thought. *"God, he's pretty."*

"Yeah -- pretty *horny*," David said. "Get in there before he beats off."

"Shut up!"

Damn. Hunter had forgotten himself and spoken aloud. David would've laughed if he hadn't wanted to come so badly.

"What? I didn't say anything, dude," Justin said, blinking at Hunter. It looked to David as if Justin had nearly forgotten Hunter was still in the room.

"Uh, nothing. Come here, baby," Hunter ordered. David loved it when Hunter's voice deepened into a rumbling baritone. It made him feel an almost real shiver tickle the pit of his belly.

Justin walked into Hunter's arms, and began rubbing his body against Hunter's tight abdomen and broad chest.

David sucked in his breath -- or reasonable facsimile thereof -- preparing himself for the onslaught of emotions and physical feelings he knew were about to assail him. It didn't start slowly, or gradually build in intensity. No, when the floodgate between himself and Hunter opened, the waves of emotions hit David with the force of a baseball bat upside the head, every muscle in his body instantly snapping tight.

Searing heat brought his blood to an immediate boil as desire, powerful and sharp, sliced through him like a razor blade. Bolts of pleasure, potent and raw, sizzled in the very core of his being and exploded in each of his cells. His hand moving over his cock was almost an afterthought, done despite the dizzying cascade of sensations rather than because of them. It was only habit that made him stroke himself; he could come just by hitching on Hunter's orgasm, but it made him feel more human, more alive, to go through the motions.

It was only in moments like these that David could really feel anything at all. More than just the swell of ecstasy from an orgasm -- although that would come at the same time Hunter found his release -- David felt a full spectrum of emotions, *real* emotions, not just the shadows of them he normally experienced. They made his head swim; some were painful, some pleasant, but all carried the velvet kiss of *life*. David sucked up the good with the bad as hungrily as a junkie scoring a hit.

David felt Hunter's pleasure as Justin fell to his knees and took Hunter's cock into his mouth. David's balls filled and swelled, mirroring Hunter's body's reactions. He felt the tingle that Justin's fingers drew along Hunter's skin as he ran them over Hunter's thighs and ass.

At the same time David experienced the full spectrum of Hunter's emotions, some of which Hunter wasn't even aware he had. He suffered Hunter's guilt at using a man he didn't know for a quick fuck, felt the depths of his loneliness, and the longing for someone who was more than just a one-night stand in his life. He tasted the vestiges of Hunter's rage at Bobby Weils, his incredulity at Cooper's nighttime aerial escapades, and his fear that the murderer wouldn't be caught before he found Cooper or killed again. Deeper yet, there even after all this time, was the sorrow, the sense of loss, and deeply buried guilt that still plagued Hunter's soul over David's death.

In those brief few minutes, David felt *alive*, and remembered what it had been like to have a pulse, to be corporeal, to live and love and fuck, to hate and fear and hurt. He remembered what it was like to be human.

David watched Hunter sink to his knees on the dirty carpet, he and Justin facing each other, heard the slick sounds as they stroked each other's cocks. He felt the heat of Justin's prick against his palm, the pulse of life beneath the velvety soft foreskin. His tongue moved against his teeth, feeling the soft warmth of Justin's tongue in Hunter's mouth, and tasted Hunter's flavor on it. As Hunter threw his head back, teeth clenched tightly as he came, David's body shuddered with a powerful orgasm. His body emulated Hunter's release, spectral come spurting over his fist.

When it was over David felt drained and boneless for a few moments before those feelings faded along with all the rest, replaced by the familiar numbness, the emptiness that had been his sole companion since his death.

If he'd been capable of it, he would have been depressed.

As he watched Hunter re-dress, silent and almost broody, ignoring Justin as Justin did the same, David resolved again to discover whether it was possible for a ghost to physically touch the earthly plane. When he did, if it was achievable, he had every intention of touching Hunter in a big way.

What David told Hunter earlier was a bit of a stretch -- actually, it was an out-and-out lie. He really had no idea whether the rest of the dead community continued to prefer one sex over the other after death or not. For all he knew, if they were straight in life, they remained straight after death. Same went for being gay, or bi, or pansexual for that matter.

David had always proclaimed to self-identify as being straight before he'd died, but if he were truthful with himself -- and since he was dead, really, he didn't see the point in lying anymore -- he'd spent his life in the closet, denying feelings and an attraction he didn't understand, and feared.

There had been many nights back then when they'd been partners that David had, in the darkness of his bedroom, fantasized about Hunter, about what it would be like to kiss him, to touch him. To get naked with him and fuck him blind.

Never, not once in all their years together, had David spoken or given Hunter any indication of his innermost fantasies. He'd been ashamed of how he felt, confident his feelings were perverse and wrong, a sign of a significant weakness and a twisted mentality. He knew how many of the guys in the department felt about homosexuals, particularly how his former partner had felt about them. Their homophobic bigotry had poisoned him, and while he was ashamed of having those proclivities himself, he was secretly proud of Hunter for being out, because although Hunter *did* keep his sex life close to the vest for the most part, he'd never denied who he was. David would rather have thrown himself under a bus than confess he was attracted to another man, particularly to Hunter, but after his death, his fears died with him.

When he became a ghost, David finally saw the folly of his repressed sexuality, and saw clearly the wasted years, and the opportunities he'd missed because of it. He'd come out to himself then, and officially jumped the fence. Hell, he hadn't just *jumped* it -- he'd pole-vaulted to the other side with a perfect ten-point landing, but he'd never intended to tell Hunter. Lord knew their relationship was weird enough without adding the awkward truth of David's secret fantasies to the mix, but now it was different. If David could discover the secret of actually *touching* the physical plane...well, then, all bets were off.

He'd be on Hunter like white on snow, and to hell with what *anyone* thought.

* * * * *

Cooper didn't want to go to sleep. He lay in his bed in his Power Rangers pajamas, staring into the darkness, fighting to stay awake, but he was *so* tired, his eyelids so heavy that he couldn't keep them open no matter how hard he tried. The night sang to him from outside his window; the streetlights beckoning like dancing fairies, twinkling in the dark.

He was afraid to sleep because he was worried that he would fly in his dreams again. He knew the Bad Man, the one with the ugly face who'd seen him and frightened him, was out there somewhere in the city, doing awful things, horrible things. Cooper didn't want to see the Bad Man again, not ever.

Plus, he'd promised Mr. Ghost, the nice man who'd come with the policeman to make Bobby leave him and Mama alone, that he wouldn't fly. Mama had told him that policemen had put Bobby in jail, and that he wouldn't be coming home anymore. That had made Cooper very happy. He wanted to keep his promise to Mr. Ghost, but now he wasn't so sure if he could keep his word. The only way to make sure he didn't fly was not to sleep, but as hard as Cooper struggled to keep them open, his eyelids refused to obey.

He lost the battle at a few minutes past two in the morning, when his eyelids finally drifted closed and stayed that way.

The instant he slipped into sleep, his subconscious awakened and his dreams started.

And in his dreams, Cooper flew.

Chapter Seven

Hunter rolled over, swatting blindly at his alarm clock. Seven a.m. seemed to come earlier and earlier every goddamn day. He didn't want to get up, didn't want to leave the warmth of his bed, but he had a shitload of paperwork waiting for him downtown, not the least of which was the paper trail that would lead Bobby Weils to prison.

He groaned, forcing his head from the pillow, rubbing his hands over his face, and instantly regretted his decision to get up. A headache hammered at the back of his head, even though -- despite his original intentions -- he hadn't drunk much the night before.

It wasn't a hangover. It was *stress* that was pounding nails into his skull, and he knew it. The hand job he'd gotten from…what was his name? Jake? Jared? Oh yeah. Justin. From Justin the night before hadn't done much to ease his tension, except momentarily. The handjob had been good, but not great, and he'd felt no connection whatsoever with the bartender. He knew he wouldn't be seeing Justin again.

Even in his dreams his mind hadn't stopped working. He'd dreamed of the murders, of the killer, and of a silent little boy who could fly in his dreams, but mostly he'd dreamed of a partner who'd been dead for five years and yet hadn't had the decency to stay buried.

David.

Hunter had felt as if his heart had been shredded into useless confetti on the day David had died. It still hurt, more than Hunter was willing to admit, even though he saw David nearly every day. It was as if David's death had stolen the spark of life out of him. Hunter could picture his heart in his chest, as lifeless as David, withered and black, strung with cobwebs. David had been Hunter's partner, his friend, his brother, and Hunter had been absolutely devastated when David had been killed.

That David hadn't really left him at all didn't make much of a difference, because in a small hidden corner of his mind was the worry that David's presence was only the work of a bereaved, broken psyche. Hunter feared that he was only imagining David there, talking to him, helping him solve cases just as David always had.

It made sense, in a twisted, mentally unstable sort of way. Even the hitchhiking sex thing followed a certain kind of logic -- Hunter had always found himself attracted to David when David was alive, even though anything between them of a romantic nature had always been completely out of the question. He supposed he'd been in love with David, although he'd never allowed himself to admit to it. Maybe his grief-fragmented mind had created a new David, a gay one with whom Hunter could find the intimacy he was never allowed to experience with David while David had been alive.

He'd gone to see a therapist once, under orders from the chief, and had been cleared for duty, but there had been several times following David's death and subsequent reappearance that Hunter had been tempted to revisit the department's shrink. He'd always been able to talk himself out of going, but every once in a while, like this morning, he questioned the wisdom of those decisions.

For a split second after opening his eyes, Hunter's last dream had followed him into waking. He'd been back in that fetid, filthy apartment, helplessly watching David die.

They'd been on a routine drug bust. Nothing major, no heavy underworld players had been involved, nothing newsworthy. Their suspect had only been a low-level, two-bit, scum-sucking street hustler who'd made the mistake of targeting grade school kids as potential customers for his shit.

It should have been a cakewalk, a bust like hundreds of others they'd done during their years together, but that day something had gone horribly wrong.

Their informant had given them an address in a section of the projects that was rife with drugs and sex-for-sale. It was in a row of rundown apartment houses that sat on a narrow tract of land like a grouping of ugly brown warts. Like so many other buildings in New York, they were built so close together that a person could reach out of a window in one building and touch the building next door.

After they'd staked the place out for hours, the perp had finally returned. They'd watched him enter the building, waited a few minutes, then followed him inside, armed with the warrant for his arrest.

Four flights up a dimly lit stairwell, past drunks sleeping in puddles of piss, tired, worn-out prostitutes and hollow-eyed addicts, to a door marked 459. Guns drawn, Hunter and David had taken up places on either side of the battered entryway. A hard rap of David's knuckles on the door echoed dully in the hallway.

"Police! Open up!" David yelled. His foot came up a minute later, kicking in the door. The feeble lock gave way without much resistance and the door banged inward, loudly connecting with the wall and bouncing back. David flattened himself against the wall, eyes locking with Hunter, waiting to see if the perp opened fire.

A heartbeat had passed, then two. Silence met David's repeated shout of "Police!" David had looked into Hunter's eyes and had given him a short, sharp nod. David was going in first; Hunter would cover him. It was their established routine; they'd done it the same way hundreds of times before.

The next few minutes played out in slow motion across the screen of Hunter's memory.

David stepped through the doorway, his gun in his hands, Hunter a heartbeat behind him. Shots rang out, three loud pops in rapid succession. The perp was knocked off his feet, his gun falling from his hand, a thin line of gray smoke curling from the muzzle. David dropped his weapon, sinking to his knees then slowly slumped face down on the floor.

A puddle of thick crimson soaked the dirty beige carpeting under David's midsection.

Hunter felt the familiar wave of guilt wash over him, black and choking. "Survivor Syndrome," the department shrink had called it the first -- and only -- time Hunter had gone to see her. *"It's not your fault that David died and you lived,"* she'd said. *"It could have been the other way around."*

Even David kept telling Hunter that he wasn't to blame, that it could have just as easily been Hunter who'd been killed. It was fate, David said.

Hunter's fear, although he didn't speak of it, not even to David, was that it hadn't been fate -- it had been *cowardice* that had let him stand back and had put David in the line of fire. He should never have been content to let David take the risk time and time again, and to hell with the fact that David had more seniority and experience than Hunter. In the beginning that had been true, but not then, not more than ten years later.

In Hunter's mind it had been spinelessness on his part, and a complacent attitude. He'd allowed it to continue because it was easy, the way it had been almost since the very beginning. The first few months they'd been partners, Hunter had elbowed David out of the way and gone in first, eager and ready to face danger, to prove himself, but he'd let David put the kibosh on his actions. David had seniority; David had insisted he would go in first. Because of that mind-set, because Hunter had never had the balls to stand up to David and insist he go in first instead, David was dead.

"Quarter for your thoughts."

Hunter looked up to see David standing by the door to the bedroom. "Penny. It's a penny for your thoughts."

"Adjusted for inflation," David grinned. "Fun night, huh?"

"Yeah, it was a blast," Hunter replied dryly.

"What's wrong?"

"Nothing. Hangover," Hunter lied.

David obviously didn't believe him, but Hunter was saved being given the third degree when his cell phone trilled. He flipped it open. "Hunter."

"Detective Hunter? There's something wrong with Cooper! Please, please help me!"

Hunter recognized Emma Weils' voice. She sounded panicked, frightened out of her wits. "What do you mean, Mrs. Weils? Where is Cooper? Is he hurt? Is he breathing?"

"He won't wake up! I called him and shook him, but he won't open his eyes!"

"Hang up and call 911, Mrs. Weils. I'm on my way." Hunter snapped his phone shut and jumped up, pulling on his pants. No time for a shower or shave. Emma Weils had sounded terrified.

"Is something wrong with Cooper?" David asked as Hunter snagged a clean shirt from the closet and shrugged into it.

"Yeah. His mother said that he won't wake up. I told her to call 911, but you know what the response time is in that area. I'm heading over there now."

"Shit! If he went flying again and met up with the killer…"

"I'm still not convinced any of that crap is true. I don't know *what's* going on, but I'm going to find out. You coming?"

"Duh."

Yeah, Hunter should have known better than to ask. Actually, this was one of the few times that Hunter was grateful to have David come along. Flying kids and ghostly serial killers were outside the boundaries of Hunter's expertise. More than ever, Hunter hoped that David wasn't just a byproduct of his grief. He needed David to be *real*, to be a ghost, and to help him help Cooper.

* * * * *

Although Hunter pressed the pedal to the metal all the way up to the address off Eleventh Avenue at Forty-sixth Street, cutting in and out of traffic like a madman, running red lights and stop signs, it still took them a full fifteen minutes to get there.

Paramedics had not yet arrived when David and Hunter pulled up to the curb in front of the Weils' apartment house, just as Hunter had predicted. That wasn't extraordinary -- seriously understaffed, it sometimes took thirty minutes or more for a response, depending on how many calls for help had come in at the same time, and the nature of the emergency.

The bruises on Emma Weils' face had deepened into dark purple and one eye was swollen shut, but it wasn't pain that David saw in her expression -- it was terror. Whatever was happening with Cooper had frightened her badly. He didn't stay to listen to her frantic explanations as she opened the door for Hunter, instead slipping past her through the living room and down the hallway. There were only two bedrooms in the small apartment, and he found Cooper's on the first try.

A blanket covered Cooper's small, thin body on the narrow twin bed, only his soft blond curls peeking out. He lay curled up tightly on his side in the fetal position, knees pulled to his chest and hands tucked under his chin. Every so often his body would tremble, but his eyes remained closed. David noticed that Cooper's eyeballs were moving rapidly behind his closed eyelids. He was dreaming, and David worried about who Cooper might have flown into this time.

"Hey, Coop," David said softly, sitting down on the edge of Cooper's bed. "Wake up, Cooper. It's me, the ghost policeman. Remember me from yesterday? I came to see you, buddy. Come on, Cooper…look at me."

Cooper's eyes remained closed. He gave no indication that he had heard David, although he shuddered again.

Emma led Hunter into the room. She reached past David as if he weren't there, which of course, made sense, since she couldn't see him. "Look," she said to Hunter, drawing down the blanket that had covered Cooper. She lifted the top of Cooper's pajamas.

His small, rounded belly was crisscrossed with long, thin red scratches. Emma pulled up his pants legs to show more of same sort of marks on his legs.

Wherever Cooper was in his dreams, he was being hurt. He looked as though he'd been whipped.

"What's wrong with him, Detective?" Emma asked, her voice thin, teetering on the edge of hysteria. "Why won't he wake up? Who's hurting him? Make him wake up, please!"

"Emma, go to the front door and wait for the paramedics to get here," Hunter ordered sharply, his voice tight with anger. David watched Emma's face pale even further, but she didn't argue, turning and doing as he'd asked, leaving them alone in the room with Cooper.

"David? Got any ideas?"

"No. He won't answer me."

"What do you think is going on?"

"Don't know. What's your take?"

"It wouldn't be the first time a mother hurt her own child…" Hunter said through clenched teeth.

"No, forget it, Hunter. You saw Emma. She wasn't faking it. She's terrified."

"Well, it couldn't have been Bobby. He's still cooling his heels in lockup. We've both seen Munchausen-by-proxy mothers who've killed their own children, yet would have passed lie detector tests. Besides her, who's left?"

"I hate to say it, but he must have gone flying again and found the killer."

"Oh come on! You don't think that the killer is --"

"I don't know, Hunter, but those marks didn't get there by themselves." David traced the snaking red marks that covered Cooper's skinny legs with his finger. "Somebody whipped this kid, and I don't believe it was his mother."

Suddenly, Cooper arched off the bed, his mouth open in a silent scream. A fresh, thin red welt rose up against the pale flesh of his left leg.

"Shit! You must be right. The fucker's hurting him, David!" Hunter swore, banging his fist against the headboard of Cooper's bed, hard enough to shake the frame. David ground his teeth, tapping into Hunter's frustration, feeling as if it were his own. "Can't you do anything? Get inside his head?"

"Don't you think I've tried? It's like hitting my skull against a brick wall. It's Cooper who spoke to me in *my* head, not the other way around!"

"There has to be *something* we can do!" Hunter growled. There was a storm brewing in Hunter's eyes, churning under his sleek brows. David had to back off from their connection -- Hunter was close to losing control, a state of being that David had rarely seen in the eleven years he'd known the man. When Hunter's temper blew, you'd best be in the next county if you wanted to avoid the fallout. David might want to hitchhike on Hunter's emotions, but he'd gladly pass on that one.

David was about to speak again when a small groan, brittle and tissue-thin, caught his ear. "Listen! I think he's coming around!"

To David's astonishment, a ghostly imitation of Cooper, pale and wraithlike, drifted through the wall and hovered over Cooper's bed for a moment before sinking into Cooper's body, like water into a sponge.

"Holy fuck," David breathed. He'd never seen anything like it before. "Did you see that?"

Hunter didn't answer, but the look on his face told David he had.

David had no time to ponder the strange vision, because suddenly Cooper's eyes flashed open, huge and bright blue, as he sat bolt upright in bed. His fingers clutched at the blanket like claws, as if he were trying to hold on to reality to keep from being sucked back into his dream.

"Cooper? Cooper, buddy, it's okay. You're safe now," Hunter said, gathering the boy into his arms. David felt Hunter's relief flood through him, the anger draining away.

"Cooper, where have you been? Can you tell us?" David asked gently. He could hear sirens outside, coming closer. The paramedics would be there any minute, and would whisk Cooper away. There would be an inquiry, David was sure. Family Services would be called in; there might be accusations of abuse levied against Emma. It was going to be one royal, fucked-up mess. Even if Hunter swore he saw the marks appear on their own, no one was going to believe him.

"I'm sorry! I'm sorry! I tried not to fall asleep!" Cooper's voice rang in David's head, his fear and pain cutting through David like a knife.

"It's okay, Cooper. It's not your fault. I know that you tried. Where did you go?" David needed to calm the boy down, get the details while they were fresh in Cooper's mind.

"I w-went flying to the zoo. I-I like it there. My m-mom takes me sometimes. I like the p-p-polar bears."

"What happened at the zoo?" David pressed. He could hear voices at the door as Emma opened it for the paramedics.

"He was there! The B-Bad Man. He...took me."

"Where did he take you, Cooper?"

"I want my Mama!" Cooper cried. Although he never made a sound, fat tears finally found their way through his shock and fear, rolling over his cheeks.

"She's coming, buddy. Where did the Bad Man take you?" He hated to press Cooper, but they needed answers desperately if there were to be any chance at all of him and Hunter protecting Cooper.

Before he could get Cooper to answer him, the paramedics poured into the room, pushing Hunter to the side, taking Cooper away from him. They settled over Cooper's small trembling body like a flock of large, white-clad birds.

"Cooper? Cooper, please think! Where did the Bad Man take you?" David cried, raising his voice over the noise of the response team, trying to keep Cooper's mind focused as the paramedics worked.

"It was a boat. A big boat and it was dark and cold! He hurt me! Mama! I want my Mama!" Cooper begged.

"She's here, buddy. It's okay now. You'll be okay." Goddamn it! David felt the buzz of Hunter's anger building again, distracting David. "Hunter, get a grip. I can't focus if you're going nuclear on me."

"Where will you take him?" Hunter asked the paramedics. "Just for the record," he said, flashing his badge, "His mother didn't do this to him. I want that noted when you bring him in."

"St. Luke's is closest. I'll mark it on the chart, but you know how it goes, Detective," one of the paramedics said. "The kid's been beaten. They'll have to call in DCF."

"If they have any questions, tell them to call me." Hunter handed over one of his business cards. "Emma, you go with Cooper in the ambulance. I'll meet you at the hospital."

Emma nodded as she sank onto the side of the bed, Cooper's arms clamping around her neck, his small face buried against her neck. "Cooper, oh, Cooper!" she cried, rocking him.

David stood next to Hunter as they watched the paramedics pry Cooper from Emma's arms and lay him on a gurney, strapping him down. She was oblivious to everyone around her. Emma's attention was focused solely on Cooper -- she didn't speak again as she followed the gurney out of the apartment to the waiting ambulance.

"We'll have to go with them," David said as Hunter locked the apartment door from the inside and closed it behind him. "You're going to need to talk to the doctors, convince them that Emma didn't have anything to do with this. She doesn't deserve the sort of shit storm from the Department of Children and Families that's going to come down on her head. Plus, if they sedate Cooper, he'll go flying again, Hunter. I have to be there if he does. I'm the only one who can talk to him, the only one who can protect him."

"I feel so fucking useless! How do we fight something like this?" Hunter's anger was throbbing beneath his skin like a living beast. It was all David could do not to suck it in and chew on it.

"Well, being pissed off like this sure as shit won't help. You need to get a grip, Hunter. I can't concentrate when you're going ballistic, and we have work to do."

He felt Hunter's anger ebb a bit. When Hunter nodded his head without argument, he followed Hunter outside to the ugly green Dodge.

Chapter Eight

Hunter hated hospitals. He hated the smells of disinfectant and disease, the sounds of machines mixing with moans of pain, the hushed tones of the staff and visitors, the hollowed eyes of the adults and the frightened eyes of the kids.

The last time he'd been inside a hospital emergency room had been the night David had died. Arguably the worst night of Hunter's life, the memories came back thick and fast the moment he stepped through the automatic sliding doors into the ER. The past intruded on the present, transporting him back to that horrible night.

Harried nurses tried pushing Hunter away, but he refused to leave. Doctors barked orders, tubes, syringes, and gauze passing hand to hand around him. David lay unnaturally still on a stretcher just out of Hunter's reach, bleeding copiously.

Pushed none-too-gently to the side, Hunter stared at David's left foot, bare, his shoes and socks having been removed the moment paramedics delivered David into the ER. Hunter's thoughts were a jumbled mess. David would be okay. God, he was bleeding so badly! Hunter would need to stop by David's place to get him clean clothes. Why wasn't he moving? David was

going to be pissed if the nurses lost his shoes.

The voices of the nurses and doctors buzzed in Hunter's ears, suddenly unintelligible.

Hunter watched a drop of blood drip down from the gurney. It formed a single, bright red spot

on the white tile floor.

The irritating whine of the heart monitor as it flat-lined seemed so loud it drowned out all

the other noises in the ER. The flurry of activity as doctor tried to revive David, doing CPR,

ordering medication, using the defibrillator was a blur of movement, barely comprehended.

Then, finally, the sympathetic eyes of the nurses as they turned away from David's stretcher

pierced Hunter. His mind refused to make sense of the studied, compassionate words of the

doctors as they told Hunter that they'd done all they could, they were sorry, but David was dead.

Then the pain rushed in so suddenly, so fiercely, it stole Hunter's breath away and

brought him to his knees, and the sob that broke free from his throat was the death knell of his

heart.

"You okay?" David asked.

Hunter swiped a shaking hand over his face and gave a small nod. The emptiness, the

blackness, receded. He needed to look after Cooper, he reminded himself, not waste another

minute reliving the pain of the past. Shaking off the memories that had frozen him just inside the

doors, he clipped his detective's badge to his lapel, and wound his way through the labyrinth of

curtained cubicles that made up the bulk of the ER, searching for Emma and Cooper.

He found them in the last cubicle along the far back wall. Emma was sitting on the bed,

holding Cooper in her arms. His face was buried against her neck, skinny arms and legs wrapped around her body. Cooper was dressed in a hospital gown already, and Hunter could see thin red marks streaking his skin through the opening at the back.

Hunter ground his teeth, his hands clenching into rock-hard fists. When he got his mitts on whoever did this to Cooper, he resolved, there wouldn't be enough pieces left of him or her to fill a cigar box. For the first time, he prayed the killer was alive, not just so that it would be easier for him to believe, or to apprehend, but because he wanted to have the pleasure of killing the bastard.

Emma turned eyes luminous with tears at Hunter. "This is my fault, all of it," she whispered. Her voice was ragged with pain. "I did this to him."

Hunter felt his heart seize in his chest. Was it even possible? Had he been too flamboozled by the hoodoo of ghosts and astral projection to see the real cause behind Cooper's injuries? Too horrified that a mother could hurt her own child that he'd rather find a supernatural cause rather than see the abysmal truth? "What do you mean, Emma?"

"I…had bad thoughts. I brought this on him." She laid her cheek on the top of Cooper's head, her tears wetting his hair. "Sometimes I wished he'd never been born, not like this. That's awful for a mother to think, isn't it? I never meant it, though! Not really. I love Cooper, and now he's being punished because I wasn't a good enough mother. *We're* being punished."

Hunter sighed with relief. She wasn't thinking clearly, and in trying to find a rational explanation, was blaming the most convenient party -- herself. "No, it's not your fault, Emma. I promise you, I'll find who's doing this to Cooper and stop them. I swear it. For now, you have to be strong for the both of you, and stop thinking like that."

Emma didn't look convinced, but she nodded.

"You'd better go talk to the nurses and the cops, Hunter, before they call DCF. They're going to think the same thing, that Emma did this, and they won't be as easy to persuade otherwise." David's voice again jarred Hunter, and reminded him of what needed to be done. "I'll stay with Cooper."

Hunter gave David a curt nod and strode across the hall to the nurses' station, where several women in white had their heads together, eyes cutting frequently to the cubicle where Emma sat with Cooper. No doubt they were discussing the marks on Cooper's body and the possibility that the woman who held him had put them there. Two uniforms stood next to them, one of them writing diligently into a small notepad.

Pointing to his badge as he neared them, Hunter introduced himself. "You're Madison, aren't you?" he asked the cop who held the notebook. "I remember you from the Benevolent Society Ball last year." He didn't mention that he also remembered seeing Madison at Feathers, but from the expression on Madison's face, it wasn't necessary. The young cop shifted nervously on his feet -- he wasn't out, and was worried that Hunter would say too much. *Good.* Hunter could use all the leverage he could get to keep them from calling in the Department of Children and Families. Not that he'd ever intentionally out a fellow officer, but young Madison didn't need to know that.

"Forget about the mother as a possible suspect. She didn't do this to Cooper. I don't know how he got the marks, but I *do* know that she had nothing to do with it," Hunter said, relieving Madison of his notebook. He glanced down, and saw that Madison had written Emma's name down, and had circled it, adding a question mark next to it.

"They look like whip marks to me, Detective," Madison's partner, an equally young, serious-faced uniform said.

"I know what they look like, but I'm telling you that Emma Weils isn't the one who put them there."

The two cops exchanged a glance. "How do you know? Were you there when it happened?" Madison asked.

Careful, Hunter told himself. *Saying too much will earn you a trip downtown in handcuffs if they think you had anything to do with what happened to Cooper.*

"Because I had Emma out in the kitchen, and when we returned to Cooper's room, there were more marks on him than before." Hunter was fudging the truth, but he couldn't very well tell the uniforms about ghostly serial killers and flying kids, or that he'd personally witnessed marks rising on Cooper's skin without any visible cause.

"You think the kid did it to himself?" Madison asked. He looked at his partner. "It could be, I suppose, but I doubt it. We've never had cutters that young before. And what did he use to reach his back? I'm sorry, Detective, but the whole thing looks fishy. We're supposed to call in DCF when --"

"I know, I know, but I was *there*, Madison. I saw it with my own eyes."

"What were you doing there, Detective? How do you know Emma Weils?"

Standard enough question, but it irritated Hunter nonetheless. "I met Mrs. Weils in the process of investigating a murder that occurred near their home." He neglected to tell them about Bobby Weils. No sense in muddying the already murky waters surrounding the case. It would come up soon enough.

"Oh yeah, that was the bludgeoning with the PVC pipe, right?" Madison asked, taking back his notebook. "Lucky break Mendoza had on that case this afternoon, huh?"

"What?" Hunter blinked, unsure of what Madison was talking about. Carlos Mendoza? He was another detective at the precinct, a short, scruffy guy with more attitude than brains, in Hunter's opinion. What did Mendoza have to do with the murder?

"Didn't you hear? Mendoza collared the murderer, the one the papers have been calling the 'Weapon of Opportunity Killer.' Turns out, the perp is an old bum with one oar out of the water. I heard he kept talking about seeing ghosts, saying that a fucking spook killed that guy the other night in the alley. Said he saw that PVC pipe floating in the air all by its lonesome, so it had to be a ghost doing the killing. He described the way the murder happened, got all the details right, down to what the victim was wearing. They're holding him at Bellevue."

Oh, the shit just keeps getting fresher and deeper, doesn't it? "This old guy -- did he have any facial scars or burns?"

"Huh? No, none that I've heard about. Why?"

"It's nothing. Never mind. Thanks, Madison. Listen, about this Weils case...I'd appreciate it if you'd hold off on DCF, just for a little while, okay?"

"I guess we can wait until morning at least. Kid's not going anywhere, and the mother will be watched."

"Thanks," Hunter said. He turned back toward Cooper's cubicle, his mind whirling with questions. Who was this old guy Mendoza arrested? Certainly not the killer -- Cooper had been very specific in his description of the killer's scarred face. If Cooper's story was to be believed -- and Hunter had seen far too much weird shit already not to, including the mysteriously appearing whip marks on Cooper's skin -- then Mendoza had nabbed the wrong guy. The killer was still out there, and an innocent man was locked up in Bellevue.

Damn it! Hunter pinched the bridge of his nose as he felt another whopper of a headache coming on.

He stalked back to the cubicle and spent the next five and a half hours waiting as the doctors put Cooper through a battery of tests, all of which came back normal. Except for being mute and autistic, and his skin welted to bloody hell and back, Cooper was in perfect health.

Someone called in DCF despite Hunter's efforts to keep the department out of it. Hunter suspected the nurses, but really couldn't blame them for doing so. To the uninformed eye, Cooper was a victim of abuse. Hunter puffed out his cheeks and blew the air out slowly, trying to rein in his temper. A conflict with Child Services was the last thing he needed at the moment, but Cooper being taken away and put into the custody of the state, and Emma Weils arrested, would only complicate matters exponentially. He couldn't allow that to happen, not only for Emma's sake, but for Cooper's.

The woman who introduced herself as Carol Hedges, an intake caseworker for DCF, was a no-nonsense person who immediately tried to wrestle control of the situation from Hunter. Out of options, Hunter resorted to scraping the bottom of his barrel of ethics to get her to agree to a conference with Emma and him before filing any reports.

He flirted with her -- openly, ridiculously, and without the least shred of dignity.

That David wouldn't stop snickering at him, and making snide comments that only made Hunter's headache worse.

It worked, though. Ms. Hedges finally gave in, blushing, and led Hunter and Emma out into a tiny office near the nurses' desk. For the next hour and forty-five minutes, Hunter's tongue danced in circles around the truth, proving the old adage to be true: *If you can't dazzle them with your brilliance, baffle them with your bullshit.*

In the end, she agreed to leave Cooper with Emma while Cooper was recuperating in the controlled environment of the hospital if Emma would agree to a psychiatric consult. If -- and only if -- the shrink thought it in Cooper's best interest to go home with Emma, then Hedges would allow it, and follow up with a series of home inspections. It wasn't the best outcome Hunter could have hoped for -- there would still be a report written and a caseworker assigned -- but it was better than the alternative.

* * * * *

A nurse came into Cooper's cubicle shortly after Hunter left with Emma and the woman from DCF. She held up a syringe, filling it with a colorless liquid from a small vial, and tapped it to rid it of any air bubbles.

David cringed as she stuck Cooper with it in his hip, although the boy never uttered a sound. Why they felt the need to sedate a kid who was practically catatonic to begin with was beyond David's reckoning. There was nothing he could do about it though, except sit next to Cooper and watch him carefully, desperately hoping that he would be able to communicate with the astral-Cooper if he went flying again.

At first, there was no change in the child. Cooper's eyes drifted closed moments after the nurse gave him the injection, long lashes brushing his rounded cheeks. His body relaxed, and his breathing grew deep and even, but there was no sign of his astral projection.

David tried to pull the blanket up over Cooper's small body, but as usual, his fingers passed through it. He turned away, feeling a dull ache of irritation (which he knew would've been a sharp stab had he been alive, which only added to his frustration) at his inability to touch the earthly plane, and again wondered how the killer managed to do it. Suddenly, he caught something moving out of the corner of his eye.

Although he'd seen Cooper's astral projection earlier, David was still startled to see *two* Coopers on the bed -- one lying down, sleeping, and the other sitting up, wide awake. The sleeping Cooper wore a thin, blue hospital gown; the one sitting up was paler, almost insubstantial, and wore his familiar Power Rangers pajamas. Astral-Cooper had a slight glow about him too, but other than those small differences, the two Coopers were identical. The pajamas covered most of astral-Cooper's body, leading David to wonder if he bore the same welts as physical-Cooper. It seemed likely to David. Whatever befell astral-Cooper also happened to physical-Cooper.

"Cooper?" David asked, careful not to make any sudden moves that might startle the astral projection back into Cooper's body.

"Hello, Mr. Ghost." Astral-Cooper spoke as easily as any other child, his lips moving to form the words. David heard him with his ears -- at least, he *thought* he did. It was a little difficult to tell, but he smiled as he realized that astral-Cooper could see and hear him.

"Hi, Cooper. How are you feeling?"

"Fine. I want to go flying. Are you mad?"

"No, Coop. I'm not mad."

"'Cause you said not to go flying."

"I know I did, but I'm not angry, kid. It's okay. Mind if I come along this time? I always wanted to go flying."

"Sure!" Astral-Cooper seemed excited, a broad smile dimpling his cheeks. "Nobody ever wanted to go flying with me before! Can we go to the zoo?"

"Why not? Oh, Cooper, before we go, is it okay if I ask you a couple of questions?" He waited for astral-Cooper's nod. "How did you get those scratches, Cooper?"

Astral-Cooper looked confused, cocking his head to the side. Then, as if he'd suddenly dredged up half-forgotten memories from some deeply buried place, his eyes grew as wide as saucers. "He did it. The Bad Man. He caught me."

"You said he took you on a boat. Do you think you could find it again, Cooper?"

Astral-Cooper shivered. "He wanted to hurt me more, make me dead, but he couldn't."

Of course he couldn't, David thought. *That fits right in with my theory!* Cooper wouldn't have been angry -- he would have been frightened. It was the wrong sort of emotional juice. The ghost killer needed to siphon *anger* in order to produce a killing rage. All he'd been able to do was give Cooper the welts. *Fucking bastard, hurting little kids. I'd like to show him what pain feels like by pulling his tongue out through his asshole.* "Do you remember where the big boat is, Coop?" he asked again.

Astral-Cooper nodded, his eyes growing even larger, filling with fear. "But I don't want to go back there. Please don't make me go back!"

"You only need to show me where the boat is, so I can catch the Bad Man. You don't have to go aboard it again, and I'll be with you the whole time. I promise. Then after you show me, we can go to the zoo." *Please kid, work with me. I need to find this guy!*

"Promise?"

"Yup. Cross my heart. I won't let the Bad Man near you, Coop." He fervently hoped he wasn't lying to the kid.

Another small, apprehensive nod from astral-Cooper made David breathe a sigh of relief -- or as near to one as he could manage without having functional lungs or emotions. "Okay, Coop. Let's go!"

He watched as astral-Cooper floated effortlessly up into the air, hovering about five feet off the floor like a pale Peter Pan in footie pajamas, while his physical self remained unmoving on the bed. It was the damnedest thing David has ever seen, and that was saying something. He'd witnessed a lot of weird shit since he'd died, but astral-Cooper's little trick beat everything else hands down.

Cooper zipped to the wall of the hospital cubicle, looking back over his shoulder at David. "Come on!" he called, laughing merrily, his eyes sparkling with excitement, elfin and full of innocent delight.

David smiled back, a genuine grin that reflected Cooper's emotions. Cooper's happiness was so genuine, so complete that it bubbled up and spilled over, brightening the entire room like sunshine. David couldn't help but tap into it. He felt true joy fill him, edging out everything else until he felt as light and carefree as a child. *How easy it is for a child to forget about being frightened.* He wished he could be the same, and hoped desperately that he could keep his promise to Cooper, and keep Cooper safe. Rising into the air, David followed Cooper through the wall, each effortlessly melting past plasterboard, wood, and brick, and out into the star-studded night.

Chapter Nine

When Hunter returned to Cooper's room the boy was deep in a drugged sleep, his narrow chest rising and falling rhythmically. Hunter swore softly under his breath. David was nowhere to be seen. Where the hell had David gotten to? If David had gotten a lead from Cooper and gone off without saying anything to Hunter, he was going to kill David -- figuratively speaking, of course.

"Emma, you're going to stay with Cooper, aren't you?" Hunter asked. He didn't want to leave the boy alone, and needed to talk to David, but he also didn't want to waste any time. He knew before he asked the question that Emma wouldn't consider leaving Cooper's side, whether DCF was watching Cooper (and her) or not. He could check into Madison's story about Mendoza's capture of the killer. That much he could do without David's help. Madison had said that they were holding the old man at Bellevue.

"Yes. I'm not leaving him," Emma replied firmly, tenderly pushing a wisp of hair away from Cooper's forehead. "You go, Detective Vance. You find who did this to my boy."

After securing a promise from Emma to call him if there was any change at all in Cooper's condition, or if anyone on staff or from DCF harassed her, Hunter left the hospital and headed for his car. He took a deep breath of cool night air to clear his head and the hospital smell from his nose as he slid behind the wheel. The fresh air did nothing to dispel the questions that spun through his mind in a whirling dervish.

Who was the old man Mendoza had arrested? How did the old man know what had happened in the alley? Was it possible that he *was* the murderer and David was wrong about everything? Did Cooper have nothing to do with the crime at all? Had Hunter imagined the entire thing? No, he hadn't imagined seeing the scratch appear on Cooper's leg…or had he? Was he losing his mind?

He clamped his jaw tight, frowning as he pulled out of the lot and headed toward Bellevue Hospital. *Stop second-guessing yourself. You know what you saw. You know David is real. You're not crazy! It's not all in your head!* He *had* to believe that, or he'd end up in the bed next to Mendoza's prisoner, drinking Lithium cocktails.

Damn David for disappearing. Hunter needed David to feel grounded, to reassure Hunter that he hadn't completely lost his marbles. The longer Hunter was away from David's presence, the more he began to doubt his sanity.

Bellevue Hospital rose up over First Avenue like a brown mountain, a collection of buildings that had begun as an almshouse in 1736 and had evolved into a state-of-the-art facility renowned for its mental health care, among other specialties. Hunter pulled his car to the curb in front of the main lobby, flashing his identification to the grimacing attendant. Let them try to tow his car -- in his current mood Hunter would gladly shove the tow bar up the attendant's ass, and sideways, given half the chance.

He stopped at the main desk and asked for directions from a blue-haired woman of advanced age, who wore a pink, pinstriped jacket and a bright Fixodent smile. She told him she was sorry, but visiting hours were over for the evening. Hunter's badge, proffered along with his patented "don't fuck with me" scowl was enough to drain the rainbows right out of her grandmotherly ass. Her smile grew icy as she gave him directions in a curt, schoolmarm voice. Hunter could read her opinion of anyone who would visit a hospital to interrogate patients after regular visiting hours in her suddenly chilled manner -- not that he gave two shits about what she thought of him. She handed him a temporary, self-stick visitor's badge that she insisted he wear.

Hunter snatched it from her fingers, smacking it onto his chest just over his heart. It sat there at an odd angle with the lettering upside down as he turned and stalked away.

Once again he found himself in a hospital, assaulted by the smells and sounds he'd come to loathe. Twice in one day was two times too many, as far as Hunter was concerned, and his face showed his distaste for his surroundings. Nurses and doctors in white lab coats parted before him like the Red Sea before Moses, eyes cutting toward him as they no doubt wondered whether he was already a patient, or soon to become one.

He ignored them all, navigating the maze of hallways and connecting breezeways until he found the wing of the hospital where the alleged murderer was being sequestered. A uniformed cop stood sentry beside the door to Room 653. A large red tag noted that the patient was in the custody of the City of New York, was allowed no visitors, warned medical personnel that extreme caution was necessary, and to strictly follow protocol when treating him.

"Detective Hunter," he said, holding up his badge for inspection. "Is this the guy Mendoza brought in? I need to question him about the murder."

"Mendoza and his partner were already here to see him a couple of times, Detective, plus the shrink and the doctors. Nobody can get a damn thing out of the old fuck that makes a half lick of sense," the uniform said.

"I'd still like to ask him a few questions myself, if you don't mind," Hunter insisted.

"Yeah, okay, but it's not going to do you a fat wad of good, Detective. That old fart is crazier than a shithouse rat. Keeps talking about seeing ghosts killing people. Me? I think the sauce has rotted his brain. He reeked of booze when they brought him in."

"Let me be the judge of that, okay? You do your job and let me do mine."

"Yeah, sure, whatever you say. Have at him. You'll see. The guy is a fucking waste of oxygen."

"So are a lot of other people," Hunter snapped, shoving his ID wallet back into his pocket. "That doesn't make them murderers. Last I checked, *crazy* didn't equate to *guilty*. You might want to remember that, Officer…"

"Grady. Why? Do you think he didn't do it?"

"I don't know, and I *won't* know until I talk to him. What's his status, by the way?"

"Medically, I have no idea. Fleas, maybe, cirrhosis of the liver, probably. The shrink was in today. You know how it goes…if he's found competent, he'll stand trial. If not, he'll be squirreled away in some old folks' home somewhere and forgotten until he croaks," the cop said with an indifferent shrug. "My money is on him getting a nice rubber room and a pair of matching rubber pants."

Hunter resisted the urge to give Grady a lecture on compassion, and slipped the old man's chart from its holder on the door. He looked through the small square of glass in the door. The room held only one bed, occupied by one Randall Carter, according to the chart. Mr. Carter had been arrested for the murder of Jason Cromwell, and was currently in the custody of the City of New York.

So the victim had a name. Jason Cromwell. Hunter winced, remembering the bloody, battered body in the alley. A name made the victim human, with a family, friends, and a life. It made the case more personal. He forced himself to concentrate on the medical file in his hand. He'd think about the victim later -- right now, he needed his mind clear, and to remain objective.

Carter was five feet seven inches tall, weighed a hundred and twenty pounds, and was seventy-three years old. There was evidence that in some point in the past he'd had his appendix removed, and his left hip replaced. There was a note on the chart saying that although he'd been carrying no identification, his fingerprints had come up in the department's computer files. Mr. Carter had been a DUI repeat offender back in the nineties, and had served a total of six months.

Since then, Mr. Carter had gone off the radar. He'd evidently given up automobiles in favor of shopping carts and cardboard boxes. There was no known current address for him, no next of kin, no telephone number listed, and no credit cards or bank accounts.

Hunter glanced at the scarecrow dressed in a hospital gown that lay restrained to the bed. Carter was staring at the ceiling, his lips moving, whispering to himself. His eyes were wild-looking, a watery blue, and red-rimmed. His cheeks were grizzled not with gray, but white, the same color as his wispy hair, and were sunken, as if Carter had no teeth in his gums to support his face's shape. His arthritic hands clutched at the silver bed rails, his wrinkled skin so thin and parchment-like that his veins showed prominently underneath it. Bony wrists and ankles were bound to the bed by white cloth restraints. Carter's legs looked like toothpicks sticking out from under the hospital gown. His body was splotched with age marks, dark brown against ivory skin. Multicolored wires led from electrodes on his body to monitors set up neatly next to the bed. An oxygen nasal catheter distorted his red-veined nose.

The victim had been fifty years younger and forty pounds heavier than this skeletal old man who had been accused of his murder. Did the Mendoza actually think Carter could have wielded a piece of pipe with enough force to do the damage that had been done to the victim? From the looks of him, Hunter doubted Carter could swing a rolled-up newspaper with enough force to kill a fly.

Another anomaly: aside from the blemishes of old age, Carter didn't seem to have a mark on him. How could an elderly man with an artificial hip beat a healthy, young man to death and not have a single black-and-fucking-blue? It was ridiculous to think that the victim simply stood there and let his assailant beat the shit out of him without at least *trying* to fight back.

Then there was the fact that no physical evidence had been found at the scene. How did an aged man, who obviously had less than his full mental faculties, manage to pull *that* off?

It was absurd, to say the least.

"Mr. Carter?" Hunter asked softly, standing next to the guardrail of the bed. Confused eyes, full of fear and pain and lunacy blinked up at him. "I'm Detective Hunter Vance of the Midtown North Precinct. I'd like to ask you about what happened the other night."

"Ghosts. It was ghosts. Didn't do nothing. Minding my own business. Fuggin' ghosts," Carter said. As his mouth opened, Hunter confirmed that Carter had no teeth; his gums were pink, smooth, and shiny. "Don't let them get me! Don't! Keep them away!" Carter's hands pulled at his arm and leg restraints, rattling the guardrails. His voice was as thin and brittle as his body. When he began to weep, he sounded like a child.

"It's okay, Mr. Carter. I won't let them get you. You're safe here," Hunter said, hoping that he wasn't lying to the old bastard. If Carter wasn't the killer and David's theory was correct, then Carter might not be safe anywhere if the murderer chose to come after him. "Can you tell me what the ghost looked like?"

"L-like a…a *ghost*," Carter replied, pulling harder on his restraints. He became agitated again. The monitors that had been hooked up to him beeped alarmingly, the images on the LCD screens spiking. "Ain't you never seen ghost movies before? It was invisible. I told them other fellas that came in here asking. I told 'em. I saw the pipe hitting that boy. It was moving all by itself!" He seemed to run out of steam, lying still, moaning the same thing over and over again. "Ghosts! Fuggin' ghosts!"

That answered Hunter's questions. He was convinced that Carter wasn't strong enough, fast enough, or coherent enough to have perpetrated the murder, and while Carter might be one color short of the full spectrum, he was telling the truth. Carter had seen the *pipe* move, but not the killer, which is why Carter thought a ghost had killed Jason Cromwell. Carter might just be right too. David's theory that the killer was dead seemed to gain more weight. Hunter swore softly under his breath as he replaced Carter's chart in the slot on the door and slipped out of the room, nodding absently at the uniform outside.

"Told you it wouldn't do any good talking to the old geezer. Crazy as a hatter; probably has that Old Timer's disease on top of being a boozehound," Grady said with the air of someone who'd been proven right.

Hunter had to swallow the impulse to beat the arrogance out of Grady's face. He refused to give Grady the satisfaction of a response. Besides, he had more important things to think about than Grady's annoying attitude.

The same question that puzzled him earlier came back, more urgently than before. How the hell was he supposed to arrest a ghost?

How Hunter was even supposed to *find* a ghost was beyond him. Only David could help him there, and at the moment, Hunter had no idea of where to find David, either.

He left the hospital more worried than he'd been going in and with more questions, but was now convinced of one fact: somewhere in the city a *ghost* was brutally killing people, and he and David were the only ones who knew about it, and could stop it.

The foremost question was no longer whether Hunter believed. Instead, it was whether they could find and stop the ghost before he killed again, and unfortunately, he had no idea of the answer.

Chapter Ten

The first thing David noticed was that, unlike a ghost, Cooper didn't traverse space by folding or bending it. When Cooper flew, he did so in real time, covering the actual distance between two points. After the first twenty minutes of following behind Cooper as he negotiated the air between skyscrapers, the novelty wore off and David began to get antsy. There were a billion other things he could be doing with his time, including getting back to the hospital to tell Hunter about the ship. Instead he was playing Follow the Leader with a skinny little kid's astral projection who was pretending to be a glider plane.

The second thing that caught David's attention was that astral-Cooper had extremely good night vision. He moved so quickly that David winced several times, sure that Coop was going to smash into a sign or the side of a building, but Coop moved with the assurance of someone who could see clearly. Maybe it was always sunny in Coop's dreams. *It could be,* he thought. *Or maybe astral projections could see in the dark.* David had no idea of how the entire out-of-body thing worked.

Arms outstretched, Cooper soared and dived, executed loop-the-loops, laughing and shouting as if he were on a ride at an amusement park. "Come on, Mr. Ghost! Catch up!" he called, hovering for a moment like an oversized hummingbird before darting away again.

David rolled his eyes, dredged up a new batch of patience, and pushed himself a little harder, pulling up along Cooper's right-hand side. "Hey Coop, how about you show me where the boat is now?"

"Boat? Oh look! The park!" Cooper nosedived toward a large square of greenery far below, leaving David no choice but to follow.

"Cooper! Cooper, wait up!" he called as the boy outdistanced him. Rolling his eyes, David negotiated a small wrinkle in the blanket of space, popping in alongside Cooper as he skimmed the tops of the trees. "Cooper, you promised that you'd show me where the boat was that the Bad Man took you to. Remember?"

Cooper turned to look at David, frowning. "Oh yeah. I remember. I don't want to go back there. It was scary. He hurt me."

"I know, but I'll be with you this time. I'll keep you safe, Coop."

"Promise?"

"Cross my heart," David said, dragging his finger across his chest, down, up, and side to side. "We don't have to go near it, Coop. You only need to show me where it is."

Cooper's lip jutted out in a pout for a moment, his eyes round with fear, but he nodded. "Okay. I saw it before, when I flew. It's this way." He shot up into the air like a rocket, and it was all David could do to keep up.

Away toward the Hudson they flew. David realized they were very close to where Cooper lived, and where the latest murder had taken place. He wondered how Cooper managed to find his house after he went out flying…Manhattan was a huge place for such a little kid. *Maybe astral projection works on the same principle as homing pigeons. Or maybe there's some type of trail he follows that only he can see.*

The river glimmered far below them, hugging Manhattan Island on its way to the sea, the sludgy waters turned black and silver by the moonlight. Docks stretched from the shore like fingers splayed out over the water; huge vessels ranging from cruise ships to tankers rocked gently next to them.

Cooper flew to the right, stopping to hover far above a long, black freighter. He grew visibly agitated, wrapping his arms around himself as if giving himself a hug.

"Is that it? Is that the boat?" David asked him.

Cooper nodded. "Can we go now? I want to go, Mr. Ghost. Please?"

David nodded, and Cooper flew away like a shot, zipping back toward the skyscrapers. David hesitated for a moment, torn between keeping an eye on astral-Cooper and investigating the black ship far below. How could he leave if he was this close? What if the ghost killer was down there?

So what if he is? I can't do anything but look *at him!* David felt both impotent and frustrated, and hated it. *I need Hunter with me...then again,* he *can't do anything either, not if the perp is a ghost! Shit, this is as fucked up a situation as any I've ever been in.*

He looked in the direction Cooper had flown. The boy was only a tiny shape in the distance. *What if the killer isn't on the boat? What if he's out there somewhere in the city, looking for Cooper? Damn it! I can't be in two places at once! I can't take a chance that the killer will find Cooper again. I have to stay with him.* With one last look at the black ship, he tore off after Cooper.

The thought that the killer might be actively hunting Cooper brought another question to mind, one that had been gnawing at David's subconscious for a while. How did the killer find Cooper after the murder?

Once voiced, David knew the answer immediately. The same way he'd helped Hunter catch the serial killers. The killer had gotten into Cooper's head, and found out where he lived.

Which meant it was possible that the killer *also* knew about Hunter and David, and the fact that David was a ghost.

Oh, man. Hunter is going to love *this.*

"Zoo now? Okay, Mr. Ghost? You promised…" Cooper said when David caught up to him.

The last thing David wanted was to go stare at animals in the dark, but he couldn't resist Cooper's big blue eyes. He had promised, after all, and David was nothing if not a man of his word. Besides, the kid had been through so much lately that he deserved a small break from all the horrors in his young life. "Sure thing, kiddo. Let's go."

They covered the distance to the Central Park Zoo in only a few minutes. Cooper led David directly to the polar bear exhibit, which Cooper excitedly explained was his favorite.

"That one is Gus, and that other one is Ida," Cooper said, pointing first to one bear then the other. "They have a big ball they like to play with, and you should see 'em swim! If you go down those stairs over there, you can look through a big glass window to watch them underwater."

David grunted and glanced at the bears in their rocky pool enclosure, pale goliaths in the moonlight, but he was more intent on watching the area around himself and Cooper. He didn't want the killer to pull a surprise attack on the boy. If the killer had the same sort of connection with Cooper that David had with the serial killers he'd helped Hunter apprehend, then the kid would be in constant danger of an attack. The killer might know that Cooper liked to fly to the zoo.

He remembered Cooper's skinned hands and knees from the night of the murder. Had the killer gotten into Cooper's mind at the scene of the murder, or had he somehow used that tiny bit of blood Cooper had shed to track Cooper? David had used evidence at the scene to track the serial killers, almost like a bloodhound tracks a scent. It was more of a vibe than an odor, but it worked on the same principle -- no two were alike.

He'd never felt so helpless in his life…or his death. David had tried and tried to touch things over the past five years with absolutely no success. Every attempt was a dismal failure, and only served to remind David that he could never be human again. All he could ever hope for was the hitchhiking experiences, and they were only all too…

A strange thought occurred to him then, one that made him freeze in place. Until that moment, he'd never realized that he'd never tried to *touch* anything while hitchhiking, and yet he was sure that was how the killer was managing it. He slapped himself on the forehead. Why hadn't he thought of that before? Would it work for all emotions? Was it only rage and fear that allowed a ghost to reach past the veil of death, or could any emotion do the trick?

He glanced at Cooper. In the way of all children, he'd put aside the fear and pain he'd suffered and was happily chattering on about his beloved polar bears. Joy suffused his small body like a bonfire lights the night sky.

David edged closer to Cooper, not wanting to disrupt him. He felt for a connection with Cooper, and found it, instantly feeling Cooper's innocent pleasure fill him, making him smile. Although David didn't breathe, he made the effort to pretend he was holding his breath, and reached out with a hand to touch Cooper's shoulder.

And felt thin bones under his fingers.

He pulled his hand away as if burned. "Holy shit!" he gasped, staring at his hand as if he'd never seen it before. Had he imagined it, or had he actually *felt* Cooper's shoulder under his hand? Was it real, or only the power of wishful thinking?

"Mr. Ghost? Are you okay?"

The joy David had felt dimmed, and he looked into Cooper's eyes to see worry graying the happiness. "I'm fine, kid."

"You said a bad word. Bobby says that word all the time, but Mama says it's bad."

"Oh, uh, yeah, she's right. I'm sorry. I shouldn't have said it," David replied. He redirected Cooper's attention back to the bears, hoping Cooper's joy would return. He needed to try it again to make sure he hadn't imagined touching Cooper. "Um, so which one is Gus and which is Irving?"

Cooper laughed, and David felt Cooper's previous happiness warm him. "Ida. Her name is *Ida*. She's a girl bear. She's over there. Did you know polar bears live way up at the North Pole by Santa? It's real cold up there, but they don't mind. They like the cold."

"No, I didn't know that," David said absently. He reached out and purposefully placed his hand on Cooper's shoulder again.

It wasn't my imagination! He could feel Cooper's frail body under his palm. *If I can touch his astral form, could I touch his physical body if I were hitchhiking on his emotions? Of course! I was right! That is how our perp kills his victims. Each one of the three previously murdered men had anger issues. I'm willing to be the last one did too. The killer is hitchhiking on the rage of his victims, using it against them. He couldn't kill Cooper because all Cooper felt was fear, not anger. The perp couldn't work up enough of a rage to kill with only fear to work with. I have to get us back to the hospital. I have to tell Hunter!*

"Okay, Coop. I think it's time for us to head back," he said.

"But I haven't seen the snow monkeys yet. They're so cute, and then there's the sea lions, and the penguins!" Cooper's lower lip stuck out in a pout that would've been adorable had David not been in such a hurry to get back to Hunter with his discovery.

"I know, kiddo, but your mom is waiting at the hospital, remember? We wouldn't want her to worry about you, would we? She's going to want you to wake up, so she can hug you some more."

Cooper's small shoulders sagged, and David felt disappoint tinged with fear through their connection. "Okay. You're not going to tell on me, are you? Mama doesn't like when I go flying. Anyway, I didn't go outside alone this time. I was with you, but I don't think it counts."

"I won't tell. I promise," David said, solemnly crossing his heart again. He felt Cooper relax. *Thank goodness for the crossed heart. It's the kid's version of a legal document, completely unbreakable.* "Come on now. Let's go."

With a sorrowful sigh and one long last look at the polar bears, Cooper flew off in the direction of the hospital. David kept close by him, trying to keep an eye out for danger, but his mind was in turmoil.

He was confident he'd discovered the secret of touching the earthly plane, but that really didn't put them any closer to catching the killer. It did bring up another question, one that made him doubly anxious to get Hunter alone.

If he could hitchhike on Cooper's happiness and touch him, could he do the same with Hunter? Could he finally touch Hunter the way he'd wanted to for so long, and if he could, would Hunter let him?

It made sense to him. He'd never tried touching Hunter while hitchhiking on Hunter's sexual desire. He'd only tried when Hunter had been calm, or at worst, mildly annoyed. David had kept his distance during the few times Hunter's temper reared its head too. In short, he'd never experimented with touching during the times Hunter felt strong emotions.

He didn't know the answer, but he did know one thing -- he was going to find out.

The flight back to the hospital seemed to take forever, although David knew it only felt that way because he was anxious -- well, as anxious as a ghost could get, anyway -- to tell Hunter about what he'd discovered.

They found Cooper's physical body in the same cubicle in the emergency room. Evidently, no beds were available for him yet, so he hadn't been moved. That was good news for David, who hadn't been looking forward to a room-by-room search if Cooper wasn't where they'd left him, and he still didn't know if Cooper could zero in on his body using some sort of internal compass.

Emma Weils was sitting by Cooper's bed, holding his hand, and crying quietly. He wondered briefly if Cooper's physical form had tried moving around as it did normally when Cooper flew, and realized that the restraints that tied his wrists and ankles to the bed would've prevented it.

David cursed under his breath because Hunter was nowhere to be seen. Where the hell had he gotten to? He was supposed to be watching Cooper and Mrs. Weils. Now that he was certain the killer had a psychic connection with Cooper, it was imperative that Cooper and Emma not be left alone.

Cooper's astral body yawned widely. "G'night, Mr. Ghost," he said as he floated above the hospital gurney.

"Night, Cooper," David answered with a smile. He watched as Cooper's astral form settled over the small body on the bed, then melted into it seamlessly.

Cooper's body stirred, his little hands pulling at the restraints, and his mother looked up just in time to see Cooper open his eyes.

"Oh baby, you're back!" she cried, ripping at the restraints until she freed him, and then gathering him into her arms. "I knew you'd come back. I missed you, my little love!"

David felt love so pure wash over him that he instantly knew it was coming from Cooper and meant for his mother. The love of a mother and child was potent, and as he tapped into it, he reached out and touched Cooper's foot.

It felt warm and solid under his hand. It worked! He could touch the living while he hitchhiked on their emotions!

He wanted to touch Cooper again, Coop's mother too, but he forced himself to hold back. This was a private moment for the two of them, and he felt he had no right to intrude on it.

Besides, the next person he really wanted to touch was Hunter, and it wasn't in a pure, platonic manner, either.

Speaking of which, where the hell is he? David stepped outside of the cubicle, looking left and right. He finally spotted Hunter coming through the double doors from the waiting area and breathed a sigh of relief. He headed Hunter off.

"Where have you been?" he demanded.

Hunter shot him a dark look but didn't answer. There were too many people around. They'd think he was talking to himself, and that wouldn't be a good thing, particularly in a hospital. David jerked his head toward an empty cubicle, and went inside, waiting for Hunter to follow him.

Hunter put his cell phone to his ear, just in case a nurse or orderly walked in. "What?" Hunter hissed. "I heard that they made an arrest in our murder case and went to interview the perp. They had him at Bellevue. Where the hell were *you*?"

"Nobody living killed those men, Hunter."

"I know it now. The guy they arrested was a thousand years old and couldn't swat a fly let alone kill somebody with a piece of PVC pipe. You didn't answer my question. Where *were* you? I wanted you to stay here and watch Cooper."

"I *was* with Cooper -- his astral form, anyway. While you were with DCF, a nurse came in and tranked him. He went flying and I had to go with him to keep him safe. I thought you were supposed to be here watching his physical form and his mom. We *have* to work on our communication skills, Hunter."

Hunter ignored his last comment. "Have you seen them? Cooper and his mom? Are they okay?"

"Yeah, no worries. They're fine. Coop just woke up, so his mom is crying happy tears for a change. Listen, Hunter, you and I have to have a serious sit-down. I found out some very interesting stuff while I was gone," David said. "Let's go see Mrs. Weils and Cooper, then get our asses home. You are not going to believe what I found out!"

"What is it?"

"No, we have to be alone. You're going to want to hear this in the privacy of the apartment, believe me. It's huge, Hunter."

"How huge are we talking about?"

"Remember when I first appeared to you after I died, and you found out that ghosts really exist? This is going to make that little revelation seem like it was nothing more than finding out the truth about the Tooth Fairy."

Hunter opened his mouth as if to say something, but snapped it closed again just as quickly.

"Good boy. Now come on. Let's check in on Cooper and his mom so we can get going. Oh, and you're going to have to arrange for a uniform to stand guard. They can't be left alone," David said, then refused to say anything else until they reached Hunter's apartment, even though Hunter nagged, bitched, threatened, and yelled at him every inch of the way there.

Chapter Eleven

Hunter chewed on the inside of his cheek, a nervous habit he'd developed after he'd quit smoking five years ago. He never really thought about having a cancer stick anymore, but at the moment he wanted nicotine, and lots of it. Nicotine, caffeine, or booze. Maybe all three of them…and together at the same time.

Yeah, definitely all three.

He didn't know what David's revelation was going to be, but whatever it was, it must be a doozy. He'd never known David to be so secretive before, not even when David was alive. When he'd been among the breathing, David couldn't keep a secret behind his teeth with a tube of Crazy Glue and a padlock, but today he'd refused to utter a single syllable on the entire trip home.

It was just so unlike him. Usually, Hunter couldn't get David to shut up. It was extremely unsettling to not be able to get him to talk at all.

No matter how Hunter cajoled, or threatened, or begged for God's sake, David stoically ignored him, staring out of the window at the scenery.

Now they were inside his apartment, and David was pacing in front of the sofa. Back and forth, forth and back, until Hunter wanted to grab him by the scruff of the neck and force him to sit, or better yet, throttle him until he spilled his guts. Unfortunately, as it was impossible for Hunter to physically touch David, he had no option but to wait until David was good and ready to tell him whatever information it was that David was sitting on.

It was annoying, frustrating, and extremely aggravating.

Just when Hunter was sure he was going to chew clean through his cheek, David stopped pacing and looked at him.

"I was able to touch Cooper today. Really *touch* him, with my hand. For the first time since before I died, I had a physical connection with a living, breathing human being -- first with Cooper's astral-self, and then with Cooper's physical body."

Hunter blinked, then shook his head. "That is *so* not funny. Please tell me you didn't just drag my ass home while giving me the silent treatment, just so you could pull my fucking leg. You touched Cooper's astral-self? Please. Do I look like I rolled off the turnip truck yesterday? Jesus, you really know how to piss me off, don't you?"

"I'm not kidding. I'm serious Hunter. I *touched* him!" David yelled. "While you were busy making nice-nice with DCF, a nurse came into Cooper's room and tranked him. As soon as he was asleep, he went flying. I was right about him being able to alter reality. His astral form looks just like him, except it wears Coop's pajamas instead of the hospital gown, and it has *substance*. It's not like a physical body, but it's not exactly incorporeal, either. It must be tied tightly to his physical self. That's how he scraped his hands and knees, and how the killer was able to hurt him. His astral self and his physical body are so closely linked that I was able to touch him in his astral form."

David was pacing again, hands clenched tightly behind his back, which made Hunter frown. David only paced when he was very agitated about something. That was a rare occurrence while he'd been alive, and *never* since he'd been dead. David didn't *have* emotions of his own anymore. He *couldn't* be anxious, even if he tried.

So what was with all the pacing?

"Sit down, will you? You're making me dizzy," Hunter said, more for his own benefit than David's. All the pacing was making Hunter worried. Could it be true? Had David actually breach the chasm between the living and the dead? No, he told himself, it's impossible! *Isn't it?*

David seemed to grow more agitated, no doubt picking up on Hunter's growing anxiety. "He showed me the location of the boat, the one the killer took him to." When Hunter gaped and began to rise, David held up his hand. "Let me finish. I didn't go aboard. Cooper was terrified of the boat, Hunter, and with good reason. That rat bastard hurt him when Cooper was there last.

"Besides, there was no telling if the perp was still there. This was before I figured out how to touch the physical plane, so I thought it would be best if you and I went and checked it out tomorrow. I figured at the time that even if I found the perp, I'd be useless because I couldn't do anything to him."

Hunter nodded. As much as he hated to admit it, David had done the right thing. Even if the killer had been on the ship, there would've been nothing David could've done about it. If the killer was indeed a ghost who could reach beyond the veil and manipulate objects to touch the living -- which Hunter now believed after seeing the scratches appear on Cooper's body by themselves -- all it would've served was to alert the perp that they knew what and where he was, and warn him off. "Okay. Good enough. So then what happened?"

"We went to the zoo, the one in Central Park. Cooper likes it there. He took me to the polar bear exhibit. He was so happy, Hunter…and that was the key! Remember when I suggested that the killer was siphoning the victim's rage? Using it to kill them? I was right. Cooper is a little kid…he doesn't possess the kind of anger the perp would need to kill. All Cooper felt was fear, which is why the killer only hurt him instead of killing him."

"That makes sense, in a bizarre, *Twilight Zone* sort of way."

David grinned at him. "At the zoo, Cooper was *happy*. I felt it, hitchhiked on it, and when I reached out I was able to touch him!"

Hunter frowned. If he didn't know any better, he would think David was actually excited, even though he knew it was only a sham, a pretense that David kept up for appearances' sake. "Wait a minute. I thought you could only hitchhike on my emotions because we were friends."

"So did I, but I guess that's not the case. I never tried it with anyone else. I didn't think it was possible. Maybe the person has to be a psychic, or the emotion has to be so strong, so pure, that it's almost tangible. The killer didn't know his victims -- at least, not that we know. It's possible he did, of course. I don't know all the rules yet. I've only just figured it out."

"Maybe your experience with Cooper had to do with this astral projection stuff you keep talking about. You may not be able to touch anybody, you know, for real."

"Nope. Not true. I told you, I touched Cooper's physical body at the hospital just before you came back. Plus, the murder victims weren't astral projections of themselves. They were flesh and blood. They may have been psychic, though. Maybe that's how the killer picks his victims. They have to be really angry, *and* have extrasensory capabilities."

"Good point and it makes sense that he would preselect his victims. Lots of serial killers do. They have a shtick, a plan they follow when choosing victims -- college students, hitchhikers, prostitutes, whatever. Angry psychics may be our guy's meat of choice."

"Maybe, or it could just be that the victims were so angry, the killer was able to hitchhike on their rage. Which would be worse, because it would mean everyone in the city is at risk, not just psychics."

"So, where does this leave us?"

"I'm not sure. It's not going to help us catch the killer, or to protect Cooper, I guess, unless I can get a bead on the perp and get inside his head like I've done with the other serial killers we've caught. But they always left hard evidence behind that I could use to track their auras and make the connection. Plus, they were all still breathing. This one is harder to crack than a virgin's ass. Anyway, this secret I've discovered, the reason I wanted to wait until we got home…it's more of a personal thing. I mean, I just…aw, hell, Hunter. Don't you *get* what this means?"

"Evidently not. Explain it to me." His patience, razor-thin to begin with after the day he'd had, was stretched to the breaking point, and these word games David was playing weren't helping. "Personal? Personal *how*, exactly?"

David threw up his hands, and started pacing again. "Jesus, you're fucking dense. I don't remember you being this thickheaded when I was alive."

"You're really starting to piss me off again, David. Just tell me what's going on, and stop with the drama, already."

David stood still a moment, then spun around to face him. "I hitchhike on your emotions because it's the only way I can experience an orgasm. Now, maybe, I can actually have sex myself. There. Is that simple enough to understand, or do I need to get you a tutor?"

"That's it? *That's* the big announcement? You think you can get laid? Well, fuck me sideways till Sunday. Call CNN. The *New York Times*. Hell, call the Pentagon! This is news of earth-shattering proportions! Never mind the war in the Middle East, or the tsunamis and earthquakes, or terrorist bombings, or the fucking murderer we're trying to catch…David Brown may be able to get his rocks off without help! Hallelujah and amen!"

"Oh, you fucker!" David yelled. "Was there *ever* a time when you weren't such a shithead?"

Hunter noticed that David's cheeks were beginning to mottle red, like they used to do when he got angry while alive. He knew *he* was feeling angry, and realized that David must be hitching on his emotions which, for some reason, only pissed him off more. "Sure, every minute I'm not with *you*."

"Bastard! How can you be so cold? Do you have any idea of what it's been like for me? Never being able to make my own choices, having to constantly live vicariously through you? Not that you have much of a life…and by *choice*, I might add. You got the looks, the sex drive, and the functioning external organs, but you throw it all away beating off by yourself in the fucking shower, you antisocial asshole!"

Hunter shot to his feet, feeling a hot rush of anger singing through his veins. He'd had it up the eyeballs with David's whining, not to mention his offhand confession that he'd watched Hunter jack off in the shower. "At least I *have* a life. You're *dead*, remember? Except, unlike most other decent human beings, you won't lie down and stay that way!" he bellowed. "How about me, huh? Do you know what's it been like for *me*? Feeling like my sex life is a porn movie shot solely for your jack-off enjoyment? Never being able to have a relationship because I know ahead of time that it's going to be a fucking threesome?"

David's face was beet-red now, although Hunter knew it was only a reflection of his own. Fury was roiling through his veins, and he knew David was hitching on it.

"Oh yeah, you're a real martyr, all right. It's perfectly okay for you to use me to get inside the fucking psychos' heads, though. Never mind that it seriously creeps me out. Never mind that their sicko fantasies would be enough to give me nightmares. That's okay, as long as Detective Hunter Vance gets his man. But let *me* ask for a favor and it's like I'm asking you for a fucking kidney!"

"You don't *have* nightmares. You don't *sleep*. Or piss for that matter, so the kidney thing is moot," Hunter spat.

"God! Can't you stop being an asshole for one single, solitary minute? You know what I mean!"

They were standing nose to nose. Hunter was breathing hard and seeing red. He couldn't ever remember feeling so furious, especially not with David. He was positively *seething*, and what's more, he didn't know why, which only made it worse.

A little voice whispered in the back of his head that he *did* know why, but he didn't want to admit it. *He won't need you anymore,* the horrid little voice said. *He can find his own lovers now. He'll leave you again, this time for good.*

He snarled at the voice in his head. *Shut up!*

"I will *not* shut up! I may be dead, but I'm still a person, *and* your partner, and I deserve a little goddamn respect!" David roared.

Oops. Hunter didn't realize David would pick that up. He still refused to back down or apologize. "My *partner* died five years ago! *You're* only his ghost, and I'm sick to death of you constantly whining at me about it!"

"Whining? *Whining?*" David sputtered, his eyes wild. Without warning he launched himself at Hunter.

Hunter smirked, fully expecting David to pass right through him.

He didn't.

Instead, Hunter felt the impact of one hundred and eighty pounds of angry man hitting him full force, knocking him flat on his ass.

He stared into David's eyes in stunned silence as his mind tried to wrap around the miracle that had flattened him. David was lying on top of him. He could feel every inch of David's rock hard body -- hands clenching at his shoulders, a knee wedged between his thighs, flat belly and wide chest pressing against his own.

A thought occurred to him, along with a million questions: this hitchhiking thing that let David tackle him to the floor was a two-way street. *He* could feel David as if David were three-dimensional again.

If Hunter could corner the killer, get the bastard to feed off Hunter's anger, he could fight back! Could he kill the murderer, or at least send his ghost to hell?

Then the question was forced out of his mind by lips, forceful and demanding, crushing against his, and a tongue, warm, wet and insistent, angrily sweeping his mouth. They instantly cleared Hunter's mind of every thought but one.

David was kissing him.

Straight David.

Straight, *dead* David.

Chapter Twelve

What are you waiting for? This is what you've always wanted, that annoying little voice whispered in his head. *Isn't this what you used to dream about, fantasize about? David and you. David, loving you. What does it matter that he's not breathing? He's here, and he's fucking kissing you like he means it.*

Hunter's anger drained away in an instant, replaced by a desire so hot and potent that he couldn't help but gasp. His cock sprang to life so quickly it came as an ache. He groaned into David's mouth, feeling David's dick respond in kind. It pressed against Hunter's groin as hard and hot as his own.

David's kiss changed immediately, segueing swiftly from furious to hungry, although no less demanding. In a corner of Hunter's mind, he thought David must be picking up on the birth of Hunter's desire, but he paid it no mind. At the moment he didn't care why David was kissing him so passionately, only that the kiss was real, that it was happening. He didn't need to know the mechanics behind David's sudden ostensible solidity. Questioning it might make the magic disappear, and that was the last thing Hunter wanted. Instead, Hunter seized the moment and returned the kiss full force, putting every ounce of yearning he'd ever felt for David behind it.

His hands wanted to be everywhere at once, to actually touch the man he'd secretly been in love with for almost fifteen years. He realized without actually putting the feeling into words that David was the man every trick Hunter had ever taken to his bed stood in for, substituted for the man he'd thought lost forever to a bullet in that ugly, cold apartment five years ago.

Those were *David's* muscles he felt under his fingers as he skimmed over David's spine to the small of his back, and *David's* ass, the one Hunter had always admired, plump and round, in his hands. That was *David's* moan he caught with his tongue, and *David's* cock rubbing insistently against his thigh. *His* David, not a stranger Hunter pretended to be David.

Hunter heaved, rolling David over to his back without daring to break their kiss. If he broke that tenuous connection he feared David would dissipate like fog in the sunshine. Instead, he murmured into David's mouth, letting David taste his words. "Fuck…just fuck." He moaned. "I don't care how this is happening. I *want*, David."

"So fucking *take*, already," David groaned against his lips. David's hips tilted, grinding their cocks together in such sweet agony that it pulled a feral groan from Hunter's throat.

An instant later, David was naked.

Hunter had forgotten all about David's little hocus pocus magic trick that made his clothing appear or disappear in the blink of an eye. It was a handy little power to have, and Hunter was both grateful that it worked on David's temporarily corporeal form and insanely jealous that he couldn't replicate it on himself. He had to strip the hard, slow way -- manually. He hated to risk breaking their kiss, their connection, but it was either that or come in his pants.

He chose the former, only because he desperately wanted to feel David's flesh pressing against his. Had it been any other man, he simply would've let loose and been done with it, but for David, he would hold back and savor every moment of the exquisite torture. He wanted each second of their time together burned into his memory because for all he knew, it might be his one and only shot.

He kept his gaze cemented with David's as he quickly unbuttoned his shirt and tossed it aside, kicking off his shoes at the same time. He wriggled out of his pants and underwear, praying silently all the while that David wouldn't disappear in the few seconds it took Hunter to disrobe.

Only when he was finally naked and lay pressed full length against David's body did he allow himself a short sigh of relief. David was still there, still tangible. He marveled again over the miracle of touching David, over the warmth of his skin and the hardness of ropy muscle under his hands, the softness of David's lips against his own. Hunter groaned, his belly growing tight with another spike of desire.

He slipped a hand between their bellies, his fingers brushing through David's pubic hair and curling around the thick shaft at its center. David's cock burned Hunter's palm with sweet heat, making his own prick, pressed against David's thigh, twitch with jealousy.

Hunter scooted down the length of David's body, kissing it, licking it, laying a trail of love bites over his flesh. He wondered whether the small dark bruises would fade when David became incorporeal again, and hoped they wouldn't. He liked the idea of David wearing his marks. It made Hunter even harder. Mine, he thought, teasing up another bloom over David's hip.

Then David's scent hit him. It was light, barely there, only the ghost of musk and man, but it was enough to spur Hunter to even higher heights of desire. He slipped his lips over the head of David's cock and tasted bitter salt on his tongue. David's flavor filled his mouth. It was the taste of male, and unlike David's scent, was every bit as potent as any other Hunter had ever tasted, only sweeter, and instantly addictive. He drew David's cock in deeper, sucked harder, wanting more.

"Fuck, Hunter!" David's gasp sounded like both a prayer and a curse. "Suck me. Oh God, suck me hard!"

David's hips rocked, encouraging Hunter to take David in fully, until Hunter's nose brushed against crinkled hair, tickling it. He fought back the urge to scratch or sneeze, concentrating on fucking David with his mouth.

"Turn around, Hunter. I want to taste you too."

Hunter was almost surprised. Even thought he had a mouthful of David's cock, somehow the thought that David might want to pleasure him in return never entered his mind. David had been straight in life, after all. Hunter figured David might be willing to be on the receiving end, but to reciprocate?

He terminated the train of thought midstream. *Stop with the questions and just do it! Quick, before whatever miracle this is fades away!* He released David's dick only long enough to swing his leg over David's chest. Supporting his weight on his arms, he returned his full attention to David's cock.

For all of thirty seconds, that is, until he felt a hot, wet mouth on his dick. "Fuck!" he yelped, his voice sounding strangulated as a bolt of white-hot pleasure rocketed through him. Half-formed thoughts whipped through his head, ratcheting his need to previously unknown levels. *David's mouth! David's mouth on me!* He felt his orgasm begin to build, his balls swelling. "David…fuck!"

David's reply was in his head. *Suck me, Hunter. Now, do it now!*

Hunter forced himself to concentrate, and took David's cock in his mouth again, sucking hard, but another thought floated through his pleasure-glutted brain. *Could I enter him? Would it be possible? Could I fuck David, right and proper?* He moaned low and long as an image of himself sinking into David's body up to his hips and riding David hard, filled his mind.

He slipped a hand between David's thighs, urging them apart, his finger probing between David's ass cheeks. He found David's hole, his finger circling over the ridged flesh before slowly pushing inside. "Oh fuck. In you, David. I want to be inside you."

David's moan reverberated over the delicate skin of Hunter's cock. "Can't wait that long, Hunter. Want to come. Please! I need to come, Hunter. Suck me! Make me come!"

He was sorely tempted to disregard David's plea, but the need in David's voice was so sharp and painful-sounding that it finally drove any thought of delaying the inevitable from Hunter's mind. Hunter felt a wash of shame dampen his desire temporarily. *How fucking selfish are you?* Hunter chided himself silently. *You can have sex whenever you want...he can't. This may be his only chance to have a real orgasm. Don't make the poor guy suffer.* He tried not to think about the fact that it might be *his* only chance to experience the joy of sharing David's body.

With a grunt, Hunter's focus returned single-mindedly to David's cock. Hunter sucked hard and long, sliding his lips from tip to root and back again, as if trying to turn David inside out via his prick. He tasted thick drops on his tongue, his mouth instantly salivating for more.

To his dismay, David pulled away from him. Hands roughly flipped him over, and Hunter suddenly found himself on his back with David poised over him. David's eyes were dark with lust, his hand jerking his cock with purposeful movement.

Hunter watched with amazement as David came. David's face seemed lit from within as ecstasy colored his cheeks. Hunter could see the tendons in David's neck bulge like ripcords as David painted Hunter's stomach with ribbons of white.

The smell of David's sex was thick in the air, and swept away the last of Hunter's self-control. He grabbed his own dick and jerked off, crying out at the sharpness of his climax as it swept through him, arching his back from the floor.

As he floated back into himself, Hunter was filled with mixed emotions. The afterglow of truly phenomenal sex was tainted by the question of whether they'd ever be able to do it again.

He wanted to; God knew he wanted to, again and again until they were two old, dried-out husks of men with walkers and pacemakers and hearing aids, and still Hunter knew he would want to make love to David. He smiled, imagining them in a retirement home, finding out-of-the-way corners and closets and humping like two gray-furred rabbits at every opportunity.

His pretty fantasy suddenly popped like a child's balloon caught on a rusty nail. David would never grow old. Hunter would, though. If he was lucky to live long enough, Hunter's hair would go gray, both that on his head and at his groin. His muscles would lose tone, his skin would wrinkle. His bones would ache with rheumatism, his fingers would gnarl with arthritis. His eyesight would dim, and his hearing fail.

David would never look differently. In fact, David would never really *be*, not ever again. Life with David as his lover would relegate Hunter to a new sort of closet. He would forever be worried that somebody would find out, and think he was crazy. If that happened, Hunter would be drummed out of the force, maybe put in a psycho ward.

Could Hunter live with that danger? Would he want to?

He pushed the questions out of his mind with an effort. All he wanted at the moment was to enjoy the moment, treasure it. Plus, the last thing he wanted was to ruin it for David.

They lay side by side on the living room rug. Hunter's stomach was covered with his come; David's had dissipated like smoke as soon as the connection between them was broken, much like the man himself. Ghost spunk, Hunter thought wryly.

"Yeah?" David looked at him with a quirked eyebrow. "You imagined us having sex before?"

Hunter winced, realizing what he'd said. "Uh…I mean…" Damn it! What had made him say that? How could he get out of it? He didn't want David to know how he really felt all these years, did he? No, the knowledge would only complicate their already convoluted relationship. Wouldn't it?

David's curious gaze deepened into a frown. "You know, I'd just about kill right now for a cigarette and a nap. Since I can't have either of those, I'll settle for the truth, Hunter. Come on, spit it out. I think I deserve some honesty from you."

Hunter looked away for a long moment. David was right. He didn't want to lie anymore. "Maybe."

"Maybe? 'Maybe' is not an option here, Hunter. Either you fantasized about me, or you didn't."

"Yeah, I did. Okay? Happy? I was…attracted to you when you alive. There. Now you know." Hunter felt his cheeks heat and knew he was blushing, which annoyed him. Damn David for making him feel like a kid with a schoolboy crush!

There was an enigmatic smile on David's lips. "So you thought about fucking me? Cool beans. Well, while we're being truthful, I guess I owe you an apology."

"For what?" Hunter grumbled, still feeling uncomfortable with his confession.

"I lied to you before. I told you that the dead stop caring about the whole gay/straight thing, but the truth is that I don't know if they do or not. Maybe their sexual preferences remain the same after death. The truth is that I had feelings for you when I was alive, Hunter, and I still have them. I was just too chickenshit to admit to them before I croaked."

Hunter's eyebrows shot up to his hairline as the shock forced him to a sitting position despite the warm fuzzies still suffusing his system. It was the last thing he ever expected to hear David say. He'd thought he knew David as well as he knew himself, but this … "Are you fucking kidding me?"

"Nope. I was closeted big time, but at night…well, I used to think about you too."

Hunter sank back to lie on the floor, moaning as the enormity of what they'd thrown away hit him. "Oh my God, David...I never even suspected! Why didn't you tell me? I thought we were always honest with each other."

"I know, I get it, and believe me, I'm sorry for it now. I wish I'd had the balls to admit to my feelings while I was alive."

Hunter felt the first stirrings of anger nudging away his discomfort. No, you *don't* get it...I was in *love* with you, David! When you died, it just about killed me too. Now I find out that I didn't have to keep those feelings bottled up inside me all those years, always so careful not to let on how I felt, miserable beyond belief because the guy I loved didn't know -- *couldn't* know -- how I felt about him! Jesus, David!"

David frowned, obviously picking up on Hunter's surge of distress. "It wasn't easy for me, either, Hunter! I was so fucking conflicted...I wanted to tell you how I felt, but I could barely even admit to myself! I loved you too, Hunter, but I hated myself for it. How's that for pathetic?" David barked a short, mirthless laugh. "Do you want to know the truth? I *still* love you. *That's* the reason I never left after I died. The *real* reason -- not the fucking hitchhiking thing. I love you, and now I'm dead, and I can't do a fucking thing about it."

Hunter stared at the ceiling, trying to sort out the tangle of emotions that sat like a lead weight on his chest. He was as pissed off as he was shocked, depressed and yet somehow pleased, all at the same time. "Shit, we're a pair, huh? I didn't tell you because *I* thought you were straight, and you didn't tell me because *you* thought you were straight too."

David sighed. "Yeah. That about sums it up. So...the question is what do we do now?"

"What do you mean?" A sudden, sharp stab of fear pierced through the knot in Hunter's chest, and he sat up again. "You're not leaving, are you? You can't go now, David!"

"Whoa, relax, Hunter. I'm not going anywhere. Not yet. I can't leave while some maniac ghost is going around killing people. I need to make sure Cooper is safe."

Hunter gaped at him. "So, that's it? That's the *only* reason you're staying -- because of the killer and Cooper? After we collar the guy, you're gone? You finally got laid, got what you wanted, so now you can leave? God, you're such a fucking shit, David!"

David wouldn't look at him. "I *can't* stay anymore, Hunter. Don't you get it? What happened between you and me was great, a miracle maybe, and I'm only sorry we didn't get together while I was alive, but…I'm *dead*, Hunter. You're not. We can't have any kind of real relationship. After the killer is caught, I *have* to go. I can't fuck up your life anymore. I have to join the dead, and goddamn it, you have to join the living."

Hunter opened his mouth to protest, to tell David that it didn't matter to him if David was alive, dead, or the fucking Easter Bunny just as long as David stayed with him, but David was gone, disappeared into wherever cosmic middle ground he stayed in when he wasn't with Hunter.

The knot that had been sitting so heavily on Hunter's chest burst, and for the first time since David died, Hunter wept.

Chapter Thirteen

David floated aimlessly through the cotton candy fluff of space. If he could feel true emotions, he knew he'd be miserably depressed. It wasn't supposed to turn out like this. He'd waited all these years, never daring to hope he'd be able to touch Hunter, to tell Hunter how he really felt. He'd daydreamed about it, sure, all the time. In his fantasies, he and Hunter declared their love for each other and would fall into each other's arms in a tearful -- but manly, oh, always manly -- cuddle. But now that they'd actually had the opportunity to bare their souls to each other, he wished it hadn't happened at all.

Hunter loved him.

David had never suspected how Hunter felt about him, not once in all the years either before or after his death. How blind he'd been! He'd been too self-involved to see it, too busy hiding his own feelings both from Hunter and himself. Now that he knew, he believed the knowledge would've killed him if he weren't already dead. David knew now that he'd been totally selfish; saw with a clarity he'd never possessed before that he was ruining Hunter's life by staying.

The bald truth was that Hunter needed to move on; he needed a lover who had a pulse, somebody he could build a life with, and that was impossible with David.

His decision was more painful than the bullet that'd killed him. Once they caught the murderer, once David was sure Hunter and Cooper would be safe, he was going to leave. He was going to find the Light, or the hallway, or a fucking cloud, or whatever it was that existed beyond the curtain of life and go into it. Heaven or hell or void, it didn't matter to him. The only thing that mattered was Hunter and Hunter's happiness. He knew now that Hunter couldn't really live again until David was good and truly dead.

He had no destination in mind, not really, but when he slipped out of the downy nothingness of space, he found himself near Cooper's apartment house. *Poor kid. He doesn't deserve the shit hand he's been dealt. Born with problems, then that asshole Bobby makes his life miserable, and now this psycho ghost is after him. Well, once we catch the bastard, he'll finally be safe. Maybe Hunter can help Emma get Coop into that school she was talking about, so he can learn to communicate the way most people do.* He made a mental note to talk to Hunter

about it before he left -- that is, once he drummed up the courage to speak to Hunter again at all.

Right now, David didn't have the courage to face Hunter.

The streets passed in a monotonous blur as he drifted toward the river. He found himself

at the docks, staring at the bow of a long, black ship. It was the freighter where Cooper had told

David the killer ghost had taken him.

I know I told Hunter I was going to wait for him to check this out, but I'm here, now.

Might as well take a look around. Anything was better than dwelling on his thoughts about

Hunter and the painful loss of something David always wanted and barely had time to appreciate.

He floated closer to the hulking black ship. *I doubt if the perp is still here anyway, and even if he*

is, well, so what? It's not like he can hurt me or anything.

He navigated a tiny wrinkle in space and popped onto the wide deck of the ship. There

was no sign of life aboard; he wondered if the ship was even still seaworthy, or if it was

anchored permanently as some sort of floating storage yard.

He wandered along the deck toward the stern. The ship was huge, although he realized it

wasn't really black – it had only seemed that way from a distance. Up close, it was really painted

with a mix of dull colors ranging from dark grays to browns. The metal railings and walls were

spotted with the greenish patina associated with age and neglect. Rust speckled everything,

reminding David of old, dried blood. The breeze blew odd bits of garbage across the deck; soiled

and crumpled pages of old newspapers fluttered like tumbling black-and-white birds.

Choosing a door at random, he entered the interior of the ship. Here things were

relatively cleaner, but not much, the difference probably being their protection from the elements outside. Even so, dust covered everything in a fine layer and lacy spider webs festooned the corners.

He wandered here and there, looking for some sign of the killer, but found nothing tangible. It was at times like this that not having physical hands sucked. Without Hunter, there was no way to lift boxes or move debris to look for clues. Even his newfound power was useless -- he couldn't touch anything in the physical plane without strong emotions to hitchhike on.

He'd just decided that he was wasting his time and would have to return later with Hunter, when he heard a noise. Spinning around, he found himself staring at the face of a boy. No, not a boy, he corrected himself. Young man was a closer fit, although barely. The kid looked like he was barely old enough to shave, but had a hard look about the eyes that David had seen before in street thugs. It was a look that spoke of hardship, hunger, and anger, and seemed to add years to the young face.

The man was a ghost; David knew it immediately from the steady, unsurprised look in the kid's eyes. The ghost was dressed in grease-stained overalls and work boots; a dirty rag hung out of his breast pocket. As David watched, the kid removed the rag and wiped nonexistent sweat from his forehead.

"You're looking for him, ain't ye?" The young man's rough voice was out of place with his looks, and sounded as if he'd been gargling rocks. David wondered briefly whether he'd died aboard this ship.

A closer look revealed the nature of that death. His throat had been cut nearly from ear to ear. The wound gaped obscenely, like a wide, smiling second mouth beneath his chin. *If he's a suicide, he did a bang-up job of it. One clean cut, straight across the jugular. No hesitation, no false starts, and deep enough to show his spine through the wound.* "He, who?"

"Ye know who. *Him.* Went by the name o' William Gant when he was alive." The young man turned his head and spat. Ghostly spittle hit the deck then disappeared. "The same bastard what did this to me," he said, pointing to his neck.

Ah, so he was *murdered.* "I'm David Brown. I used to be a detective here in Manhattan. Who are you?"

"Abel Smith, at your service. Folks used to call me Abe. Seaman First Class aboard the *Mary Gray.*" Abe's hand caressed one of the large pieces of pipe that crisscrossed the engine room with a lover's touch. He didn't seem to notice when his fingers passed through the metal. "Finer lady has never sailed, and that's the truth. I was only aboard her for a year before I died. Damn shame how they're letting her go to rot."

"Damn shame," David echoed absently. His mind was working feverishly, trying to figure things out. Could it be that the man who murdered Abe, this William Gant, was the same serial killer he and Hunter were looking for? It seemed more than possible. After all, how many murderers could there be who frequented this particular floating junkyard?

"Murdering bastard killed twenty men before one o' the cooks nailed him with a pot o' boiling water. Scalded the skin right off that devil's face, he did. Then the cook – Hempty his name was, a big, burly man, I remember -- grabbed Gant and pressed that murderous bastard's face down on the kitchen grill and held it there while Gant fried. Gant sizzled like bacon on a hot griddle. Wasn't an easy death for Gant, sure enough, but it wasn't more than he deserved. Hempty finally finished him off with a butcher knife. I wanted to rip the bastard's heart out and feed it to the fish, but o' course I was already dead by then. Still and all, it gave me no small measure o' satisfaction, I can tell ye."

Well, that explained Cooper's description of burns on Gant's face, David thought. "This Gant…did he kill these men all at once, or was it over time?"

Abe turned his head and spat again. "Oh, he was a clever one, Gant was. At least with the first fifteen or so he murdered. Whenever we got into port and the rest of the men went drinkin' or whorin', Gant went lookin' for blood. See, to look at him you wouldn't take him for a killer. He was tall, but narrow. Skinny. Mealy-mouthed too -- I remember his mouth got him beat on a few times -- but mostly nobody paid him much mind. Gant was the kind o' man who blended in with the woodwork, if ye get my meaning.

"Anyway, as time went on, he got sloppy or stupid; it was when he started killing aboard ship that he got caught. Gordon Mass, one o' the engineers, came upon him just as he was killing Donovan Shaker. Good man, that Donovan. Used to whistle like a farkin' bird. All kinds of tunes too. He had a real talent. Could've been in vaudeville if the sea didn't get in his blood first."

Vaudeville? Jesus. Wasn't that back in the 1920's or 30's? Had Gant been killing all the time since, or had he only recently learned to hitchhike? David nodded, impatient to hear the rest of Gant's story. "You were saying about Gant…?"

"Oh aye. Well, when Gordon caught him in the act, Gant must've lost what little sense God planted in his skull. Started yelling to beat the band, bragging on how many folks he'd killed. Killed Gordon, plunged that knife o' his right through Gordon's eyes, poor bastard, then went on a rampage, is what Gant did. Ran through the ship, deck to deck, killing everybody what got too close to him until he got to the galley. The cook got finally got him." Abe laughed, his shoulders shaking. "You should've heard Gant a-screaming when his face hit that griddle! It were music to me ears."

"So, Gant comes back here to the ship now? You've seen him recently?" David asked.

"Oh aye, from time to time. I keep out o' his way. Wouldn't piss on him if he was on fire, no sir. Always up to no good, if you ask me. Business as usual for the likes of him, I suppose. Lord knows if there was any such thing as justice, Gant would be roasting in the devil's oven right now 'stead of still plaguing the earth." Another stream of ghostly spittle sailed out of Abe's mouth. "I had a girl ashore in New York, you know. Alice was her name, and she was such a pretty little thing. I joined up with the crew here so I could make enough money to marry her. We were going to get a cottage up on the coast of Maine, and I was going to be a lobsterman." A look of infinite sadness replaced the hardness in Abel's eyes for a moment, but then it passed. "That bastard Gant ruined it for me. Killed me before I could marry my sweet Alice."

"I'm sorry, Abel. That's a shame." David did feel badly for the young man, but he needed to worry about the living at the moment, not the dead. "Do you have any idea what Gant's up to now?"

"Brought a young boy with him last time he was here. How Gant managed it, I don't know. Alive the boy was, not dead like us. Anyway, this poor little fella was a-whimpering and crying for his mama. Sumbitch enjoyed hurting the lad. The rotten bastard!" Abe pounded the ship's pipe ineffectually, but didn't seem to notice his hand sliding through the metal. David knew Abe's anger was only a sham, an act performed out of habit, but had to admit Abe did a fine job of it. He was convincing, for all he was ghost and couldn't *really* be feeling any emotion. "I was afraid Gant was going to kill the lad, but then the damnedest thing happened. After a while, the boy just disappeared, like smoke."

That settles it. The killer is *Gant! The boy could only have been Cooper.* "Can you show me where Gant brought the boy?" David asked.

"Aye. Had him up in what used to be Gant's quarters. I'll show ye. It's this way."

David followed Abe up a deck and past a series of small cabins. The doors were open, and he could see some were stuffed ceiling to floor with crates; others were empty except for the skeletal, ironwork remains of bunk beds and cots, and a few thin, mildewed mattresses. They finally stopped, and Abe led the way into one of the last rooms near the bow. Abe pointed to the bottom bunk on the right. "This'n was Gant's when he was alive."

David knelt by the bunk, wishing more than ever that he could rummage through the junk piled on it. Rags, newspapers, and magazines lay in a messy heap, covering the bare, moldy box spring. He read the dates of the magazines and newspapers that he could see. There was a *New York Evening Post* from 1937, and a *Life* magazine from 1962. A postcard was stamped 1971.

David knew that if he could feel revulsion, or shiver, he would. Gant must have thought he was safe here; he'd been much more careless in this cabin than at his crime scenes. While the scenes had been clean of evidence, physical or spectral; here Gant's aura, his ectoplasmic fingerprints as it were, covered everything on the bunk. They looked black and oily, and David knew if he could smell them, they'd have a rotten stink, like gone-over meat.

He didn't want to do this, would've given anything if there were only some other way, but he knew there wasn't. He needed to get a bead on Gant, to forge a connection that would allow him to find Gant. Closing his eyes, he reached out with his mind and let it touch Gant's repulsive spectral spoor, following the gossamer-thin trail across the cosmos to its end. He hesitated, then took the next step and entered Gant's mind.

David's head was instantly filled with nightmarish images of mutilated bodies and blood. He instinctively recoiled from the horrors zapping through his brain at light speed, but forced himself to go back, to concentrate, to weed through the memories of a madman.

Dear God, how many people has this monster killed? David's mind reeled from what he was beginning to suspect was a much larger number than either he or Hunter had ever imagined. There were far more than the four murders he and Hunter were working on, certainly. More even than the twenty Abe claimed Gant had killed while he was alive. If the number of bodies flashing through his mind was an accurate representation of Gant's kills and not a psychotic's imaginary toll, then Gant had killed *hundreds* of people over the decades.

They were real. Each one of the bloody images, frozen in Gant's memory like a macabre photograph, was all that remained of a once living, breathing human being. David was sure of it.

The dizzying cavalcade of slaughter began to slow until it finally stopped. The last body David saw in his head was the young man from the murder scene in the alley. He had a glimpse of another memory; Gant's surprise at seeing Cooper near the Dumpsters, and later, Gant's sick delight and bitter frustration as he tortured Cooper in this very room but couldn't work up the juice to kill Coop.

Then David was truly inside Gant's mind. He remained completely still, concentrating on thinking nothing at all. He'd never had to get inside a ghost's head before and wasn't sure it would work in the same manner as it did with the living. What if the avenue he opened between himself and Gant was a two-way street? He would be making it easier for Gant to find Cooper, which was the last thing David wanted to do.

He felt no awareness, though, nothing to indicate Gant knew of David's presence in Gant's head. Reassured, David began to carefully poke around.

He didn't need to feel emotions to know that what he found was terrifying.

Chapter Fourteen

"His name is William Gant. He died in 1937 aboard the *Mary Gray* after killing five members of the crew. He was twenty-seven when he was killed, and in excellent physical condition, aside from being totally, completely insane, of course. Hunter, Gant's our man."

Hunter was sitting at the dining room table, morosely staring into his coffee cup when David had blinked into the room. He jumped, caught off guard. He hated when David did that popping in and out thing, and what's more, David knew it. Hell, he'd told David often enough. One would think David would take the hint and stop.

He was still angry with David because of their argument the day before, and because of David's sudden disappearance -- not to mention the life-altering truths they'd declared to each other after their round of sex, although he was trying hard not to think about *that* -- and refused to give David the satisfaction of seeing his jittery nerves. To cover his discomfort, he scowled and swiftly returned his gaze to the oily film floating at the top of his morning coffee, long gone cold. "What are you yapping about now?"

David's presence was distracting. To his chagrin, Hunter's body hardened despite his unease. It seemed that since they'd had sex, Hunter was having great difficulty keeping his head and his cock separated. His mind wanted to be pissed off; his body wanted to be buried up to his chin inside David's ass. *Well, what do you expect? You haven't gotten laid in so long, and you have to admit he* was *smoking hot. Best sex you ever had, in fact, and it was with a dead guy. Figures. I'm a glutton for punishment, and that's all there is to it. A real masochist. It's worse now that I know how he feels about me. All those years when we could've been together...wasted. Honest to Christ, my life is one long, fucking tragedy.*

"I went to the black ship --"

Hunter sputtered, jarred out of his gloomy introspection. "You did *what?* After we decided we would go there together? What the fuck is wrong with you, David? What if the killer was there? What if you scared him off?"

David glowered at him. "He wasn't and I didn't, and please try to keep your temper in check, Hunter. After everything I saw in that maniac's head, the last thing I need is to be channeling your anger right now."

Hunter snapped to attention, excitement brewing in his gut, pushing away both his anger and his self-pity. "You got into the killer's head?"

"Oh yeah, and believe me, I wish I hadn't. This guy is full-out Loony Tunes, Hunter. There wasn't a single thought in his head that wasn't severely twisted. It was…I never… Well, suffice it to say that I'd need to be tranquilized if I was still alive."

His pique evaporated, blown away by the news. "Tell me everything." he sat back in his chair, listening intently as David recounted his visit to the black ship. Hunter could tell how disturbed David was because he was pacing, but his restlessness only added weight to his statements, even if he was only picking up on the mounting excitement Hunter was feeling as David told his tale. This was the biggest break they'd had in the case since they'd discovered Cooper's extraordinary talent.

"We were right on target about the anger connection, Hunter. Gant uses his victim's emotions to hitchhike and develop the murdering frenzy he craves, but that's the *only* thing we got right. As long as the emotion is strong enough, the victim doesn't need to be psychic. The last four victims were men, but he's killed women over the years too. He doesn't do much prep work before the murders, either. When the need to kill comes over him, he takes to the streets and just wanders around until he feels anger coming from somebody. He can't carry anything with him because he can't touch anything until he's hitching, which is why he uses whatever's available as a murder weapon."

"So the papers hit the proverbial nail on its fucked-up head when they dubbed him the 'Weapon of Opportunity Killer.' Swell."

"It gets worse, Hunter."

Hunter shook his head. "Worse? How in the blue fuck can this get any worse?"

"He doesn't need nearly as much juice as he used to in the past."

Hunter jumped to his feet, squaring off against David. "What do you mean?" he asked in a low voice. Anyone who didn't know him would think he was extremely calm, and under control, but he knew David felt the fear shredding his innards. He could see it in David's eyes. Hunter couldn't hide anything he felt from David, and by now, he knew it. There was no sense in even trying.

"From what I could glean in the short time I was inside his head, it appears that the more often he kills the less anger he needs to leech in order to reach critical mass, as it were. In the beginning, the people he murdered had to be feeling a towering rage. Now they only need to feel angry. Got a parking ticket? Miss your bus? Have words with someone at work? Gant could use that twinge of anger to kill you."

"Please tell me you're shitting me, David."

"Sorry. I only wish I was."

Hunter looked out the window of the apartment, where the streetlights flickered. "Well, there's no shortage of angry people in this city, that's for sure. It wouldn't be all that difficult to find one alone, and kill him."

"It's not just in New York," David chided. "There's no shortage of angry people *anywhere*, Hunter. We're just the lucky ones that have a psycho ghost who preys on them."

"Point taken," Hunter said. He suddenly couldn't stand still another minute. He blew past David, and hurried into the bedroom, grabbing his shoulder holster and badge from the top of the dresser, and his gun from its customary place in his underwear drawer. So, what are we waiting for? We obviously don't have any more time to waste. Let's go get the bastard!"

"Hunter, wait! You're missing a few critical points, here," David said, blocking the bedroom door.

Hunter frowned at him, and walked straight through him into the living room. "What now? You got into his head, you said. That means you can find him, right?"

"Well, yeah, that's the way it usually works, but --"

"But, what?" Hunter leveled a steely glare at David. "You're not getting cold feet, are you? David, you were always the first one to charge into the room, ready to take out the bad guy. Gant can't even hurt you anymore -- you're already dead! What are you afraid of?"

"Hunter, be reasonable! I'm not afraid for me, although obviously if it turns out that you can send Gant to the hereafter, he can do the same to me. It's *you* I'm worried about. If you get killed, who'll be left to protect Cooper from this maniac? We have to take a breather, think about it, and form a plan of action."

"I've already got a plan. Look at me, David. I'm furious. When I find this bastard, he's going to leech off my emotions, right? Just like you and me last night…" His voice trailed off and he coughed uncomfortably. He hadn't meant to bring it up, but it slipped out before he could stop himself. He rushed on, hoping David wouldn't pick up on the reference. "If he can reach out to touch me, I can do the same right back to him! I can take him out, David."

"There are so many flaws in this plan of yours that I don't even know where to *begin* to point them out!" David argued. "First of all, you're not *angry* as much as you're *excited*. I can feel it, Hunter. Not that I blame you...we've been working hard on these four cases, and this is the first break we've gotten. Remember how we figured out that he couldn't kill Cooper because the kid was frightened, not angry? What if we get to Gant, and neither of you can do a damn thing but trade insults? All it would serve is to warn Gant off. If he's smart -- and unfortunately everything points to him not being stupid -- he'll take off for somewhere else, another city, even another country, and we'll lose him forever. But most importantly, if it does work and Gant goes after you, well...how do you fucking kill a *ghost*?"

"I'll send him to hell."

"Yeah? How? What's your game plan, Hunter? Do you have hell's number programmed into your phone? 'Hello, Satan? Your order of one mass murderer is ready for pick up.' Is that the plan?"

David stood between Hunter and the apartment's front door as if he could keep Hunter from leaving.

Yeah, fat chance, Casper. You're not exactly made of roadblock material anymore. Hunter glared at him.

Yet, he didn't barge past -- or through -- David, because as much as Hunter hated admitting it, he knew David was right. Again.

Hunter ground his teeth, aching to ignore David's logic and run out into the city, find Gant and end it, but he couldn't. It would only be a waste of time. He needed David to locate Gant. His only other option was to wander around aimlessly hoping Gant would find *him*, which would be about as effective as winning the lottery without buying a ticket. Besides, he knew

David was also correct about Hunter's current state of mind. He wasn't so much angry as he was energized; excited by the break in the case he'd been praying would come for so long. Still, he wasn't sure he could stand by idly now that they had an ID on the perp.

"Hunter, we have to talk about this, plan our strategy carefully," David repeated. "We may only get one shot at him."

"I know, I know! I'm not deaf. It's not like I didn't hear you the first time. I can do this, David. I'm not some rookie who doesn't know his ass from his elbow."

His bitterness seemed to go unnoticed. "What we need to do is find out if the fucker can be hurt -- or at least sent out of the mortal plane -- before we try anything, and exactly how to do it. Please, stop and think about this, will you?"

Hunter looked away, still torn by his impractical desire to run outside and do something, *anything* to end Gant's reign of terror, and logic, which demanded he listen to David, and plan accordingly.

David pressed on. "Look, let's assume you're right, that you *can* kill Gant, or at least boot his twisted ass into the hereafter. Well, that'd be great! Dandy. End of all our problems, right? But what if something goes wrong?"

Hunter spoke through gritted teeth. "Nothing will go wrong."

"Oh yeah? Like nothing went wrong on the night I was killed?"

Hunter gasped as old wounds were ripped wide open, and pain sliced through him, fresh and raw. "That was a fucking low blow, David." He noticed David flinch, and knew David had shared his pain through their connection. He was ashamed to feel a small twinge of satisfaction at the injured expression on David's face.

"I know, and believe me, I'm sorry to bring it up. I'm not trying to hurt you, Hunter. I've said before that what happened to me wasn't your fault. I only brought it up because it proves my point -- it wasn't something we *planned* on happening. Nobody *plans* on things going south for them. If we rush in there like gangbusters, we can fuck it up, and it may be the only shot we get at the bastard."

Hunter nodded slowly, giving in to his better judgment however grudgingly, his shoulders slumping. "You're right. Of course, you're right. So, what do you suggest we do? We can't just stand around with our thumbs up our asses doing nothing."

David smirked at him -- the bastard. "While I'm sorely tempted to take you up on that thumb thing, the first thing I think we should do is check on Cooper, make sure the kid and his mom are okay. Then you and I have to have a serious sit-down. Brainstorm about our options. Maybe talk to a psychic."

Hunter gaped at David, astounded and suddenly angry again. "A *psychic*? Are you nuts? You want to waste time staring into a crystal ball or having your palm read? *Now?* When we finally have a bead on the fucking killer?" David's piercing glare made Hunter realize David was hitching on Hunter's emotions again. He forced himself to calm down. "You can't be serious, David."

"Yes, I'm serious. I don't mean a self-professed, dime-store psychic, Hunter. I mean an authentic medium, somebody with experience who might be able to tell us more about the veil between life and death."

"You think some tarot reader knows more about death than *you* do? Correct me if I'm wrong, but I figured *you,* being a corpse, were the expert."

From the way David's eyes narrowed, Hunter knew he was insulted. "For the last time, don't call me that. It bothers me, okay? I *know* I'm dead. I don't need you reminding me about it every time we have an argument."

Hunter rolled his eyes. "I'm sorry, but David, this 'going to a psychic' idea would be a ridiculous waste of time."

"Why? Are you going to stand there and tell me you don't believe in life after death? Or that the line between them can be crossed? Because if you are, I feel behooved to remind you that you had sex with your dead partner last night, there's a kid we both know who can astral project, and we have a fucking ghost on the loose who seems intent on murdering the rest of the city."

"Well, no, of course I'm not saying that, but --"

"Then why is it so difficult for you believe that somebody other than yourself has any experience with the dead? As for me being the expert on all things deceased, that doesn't wash. I told you before that nobody hands you an instruction manual when you die. Everything I *do* know I learned from trial and error, and there's probably a hell of a lot I haven't figured out yet."

Hunter turned away, hemming and hawing, trying to come up with an argument, and felt irritated when he failed. David was right -- yet again -- and Hunter -- yet again -- hated to admit it. He looked back at David. "Well, suppose you're right. How are we supposed to find this expert medium? Visit every storefront psychic in the city until we strike gold? Even if it could do us some good, we don't have that kind of time."

David snorted. "We don't have to *try* to find one. We already know one."

"Who?"

"Emily Peacock. The woman the chief brought in after the second murder. You remember her?"

"Yeah, I remember. I also remember she couldn't find a goddamn thing. That's why the chief booted her off the case."

"Maybe so, but we have to take the chance. She's found missing people, and led cops to hidden bodies. I think she's the genuine article."

"Then why hasn't she found our killer?"

David shrugged. "The chief didn't give her much of a chance, and neither did you. When she couldn't help on the ball peen hammer case, she got the boot. You didn't think she could help, and weren't willing to give her the benefit of the doubt. I believe you called her a kook."

"She got tossed out on her ear because she couldn't find anything. Which brings up another good point…if she's such a great medium, how come she didn't know the killer was a ghost?"

David shrugged. "Maybe she did, but was too scared to tell you, thinking you'd never believe her. Or maybe she didn't pick up on it…might I remind you that we didn't either, not until this last murder, and even *then* it took a ghost witness and Cooper to convince us. That doesn't mean she doesn't have information we can use, Hunter."

Hunter eyed David in irritation. "Have I ever told you that I really, really hate it when you're right?"

Chapter Fifteen

After they'd left Hunter's apartment, they'd stopped in at the hospital to check on Cooper and Emma Weils. Both seemed fine. The doctors had admitted Cooper for observation, ensuring he'd be there a few days at least. DCF had backed off, at least temporarily, content in having the nurses and doctors keep a close eye on Emma's interaction with Cooper, and the policeman stationed at the door. The cop had nothing to report -- no strange noises, visitors, or anything else out of the ordinary. Cooper seemed to be sleeping peacefully, and although there was no evidence to suggest his astral form was out flying, David worried. On this point, he agreed wholeheartedly with Hunter -- they needed to catch Gant quickly, before the bastard got his hands on Cooper again.

After leaving St. Luke's, they'd taken the Lincoln Tunnel under the Hudson River to the New Jersey side. They rode in silence for the most part, neither one wanting to rekindle their earlier argument.

Emily Peacock didn't own a storefront tarot parlor, or have a neon PALMISTRY sign flickering in her living room window, as one might've expected. Her address was a small, neat Cape Cod on a quiet, tree-lined street in Bergen County, about a half-hour ride from Manhattan. There was nothing about the white, aluminum-sided house, with its picturesque window boxes full of colorful flowers, or its neatly trimmed hedges to suggest that a psychic lived within its walls.

"If she's a genuine psychic, shouldn't she already know we're here?" Hunter asked as he pulled the car to the curb and stared at the front of the house. He sounded snide, smug, as if the fact that Peacock wasn't waiting for them on her front porch with hot coffee and crullers only proved his earlier belief that she was a fake.

"You know, *you're* psychic to an extent, Hunter. You're empathic, at any rate. Can *you* tell the future?" David shot back. It rankled that Hunter refused to be more open-minded about Peacock's ability. He was sure it was just Hunter's natural bullheadedness rather than a true disbelief.

"I'm not psychic. I'm normal," Hunter said, looking affronted, just as David suspected he would.

David rolled his eyes. "For God's sake, that wasn't an insult, Hunter. If your nose was any more out of joint, you'd be sniffing your fucking hairline. Look, I don't want to argue about this anymore, okay? Let's just go talk to the lady, see what she can tell us, if anything."

"Fine."

"*Fine*," David spat back, then quickly disappeared out of the car, content -- however immaturely -- to get the last word.

He waited while Hunter took his time getting out of the car and walking up to the steps to the front door. Hunter needed to ring the doorbell twice before she finally appeared. For a minute, David thought she might not have been home. If she wasn't, he feared he'd have to lock Hunter in the trunk of the car to keep him from leaving.

Emily was a slender woman of a certain age, whose face, though beginning to show the creases time carves in all youthful skin, was still very attractive. Her blue eyes were clear, and showed the workings of a sharp mind behind them. She wore a flowing dress in a soft, flowery print that covered her from neck to ankles. Her surprise at seeing Hunter standing on her doorstep was evident in her expression when she opened the door.

"Detective Vance? What are you doing here?" she asked without preamble.

There was an edge in her voice that told David she hadn't forgiven Hunter for his cavalier treatment of her while on the scene of the ball peen hammer murder case. "Be nice," Hunter," he said. "Remember, we need her cooperation. If you piss her off, she won't help us, and we'll be screwed."

Hunter must've gotten David's point, because he'd pasted his professional smile -- not too cheeky, not too flirty -- on his face. "Um, hello, Ms. Peacock. I was wondering if I could speak to you for a moment," Hunter said.

Emily Peacock didn't seem moved either by Hunter's looks or his smile. "I don't think we have anything to say to each other."

To Hunter's credit, he remained calm and polite, even thought David could sense his irritation. "Please, Ms. Peacock. I know I owe you an apology. Things have happened since we last saw each other to convince me that I was wrong about you."

Indecision flickered in Emily's eyes. "Oh?"

"Yes, ma'am. I'm very sorry I didn't believe you at the time."

She didn't seem convinced, but at least she hadn't slammed the door in Hunter's face. That was encouraging, David thought.

"What's happened to make you change your mind?" Emily asked Hunter.

David felt Hunter's sigh all the way down to his toes, and knew it was costing Hunter greatly to talk about David to a virtual stranger. "I hardly know where to begin. My partner showing up, for one thing. My *dead* partner. He's been haunting me. He's standing next to me right now, telling me to be nice to you."

"I don't haunt you," David sniffed, although he wasn't surprised when Hunter ignored him.

Emily's eyes slid toward David briefly. David was floored when he realized that she could see him! Perhaps he'd been naïve to think Hunter was the only one who could see ghosts. It made sense that a powerful psychic might have the ability as well.

It was obvious to David that Emily knew Hunter was telling the truth, but wasn't about to let Hunter off so easily. David's respect for her inched up another notch. "Why should I believe something so fantastical?"

"Because he told me you can help us, and I trust his judgment." Hunter looked decidedly uncomfortable, shifting his weight back and forth from one foot to another, like a small boy forced to admit he'd done something wrong. "Please, Ms. Peacock, could we talk inside? What I have to ask you is incredibly important. As clichéd as it sounds, lives are at stake."

For a minute, David was sure Emily was going to say no, but then she swung the door open wider and invited them inside. He shared Hunter's relief as he followed him into the small Cape Cod.

The interior of Emily Peacock's home was the complete antithesis of the woman herself. Teetering stacks of boxes and newspapers, piled nearly to the ceiling, lined the entry hall and continued into the small living room. Narrow, maze-like corridors opened between the stacks, barely wide enough for Hunter's wide shoulders to pass through.

Interspersed among the boxes, newspapers, and magazines, were piles of stuffed animals, pots, dishes, lamps, toasters, detergent, canned goods, and mounds of other miscellaneous items.

It looked to David as if a discount warehouse had exploded in Emily Peacock's living room.

David immediately realized Emily was a hoarder, one of those disturbed people who suffered from a pathological need to save things, to collect multiples, even objects for which they had no use. He saw in a glance that Hunter was more than dismayed by the sight of the house…Hunter was clearly terrified, and nearly spun around on a heel to escape before one of the unstable stacks came raining down on their heads, burying them under an avalanche of junk.

"Keep going," David said, He tried to nudge Hunter forward, but of course, his shoulder passed right through Hunter.

Hunter scowled and shook his head. *"She's nuts,"* he thought, knowing David would pick up on it.

"She's eccentric."

Hunter jerked his chin toward a large, open cardboard box. *"Eccentric doesn't need a hundred ceramic cats. Crazy does."*

"I suppose you're wondering about my…collection," Emily said, as if she'd heard their internal conversation. She led them toward a larger opening between the stacks, where a sofa and two wingback chairs sat. "Being psychic isn't really a gift. It's a curse. I see and hear things that would make other people mad. I've found that collecting things that are tangible, that I can hold and taste and smell, gives me comfort."

"Oh, of course," Hunter replied dryly. "That makes sense."

David wondered if she were psychic enough to pick up on Hunter's sarcasm. Judging from the way she frowned at Hunter, she had.

To his relief, she didn't kick them out. He supposed she was used to people's reaction to her "collection."

"Please make yourself comfortable, Detective Vance," she said, gesturing toward the floral-printed sofa. She paused, then added, "You too, Detective Brown." She looked at Hunter. "Can I offer you a drink? Lemonade, or tea?"

Hunter looked stunned that she'd acknowledged David, but David knew better. Emily might be a hoarder, but she was also a powerful psychic. Hunter sat, his big body looking out-of-place on the small, flowery-print couch, looking loathe to touch anything with his bare skin. The house wasn't dirty, just phenomenally cluttered, but who knew what was growing in the thick of those stacks? "No, thank you."

Emily perched gracefully on a matching armchair, her hands folded on her lap, facing them. "Very well, then. Suppose you tell me why you came all the way out to Jersey to see me?"

Hunter nodded. "You remember the ball peen hammer case? The one you...helped us on?"

Emily nodded, and motioned for Hunter to continue.

Points to Hunter for not mentioning that she was thrown off the case, David thought. *And double points to Emily for not calling him on it.*

"There are three other unsolved murders similar to it in our precinct. The others also involved odd weapons -- a two-by-four, a brick, and a piece of PVC pipe -- and little to no evidence left at the scenes. We think all four murders were perpetrated by the same man." He glanced at David, swallowing visibly. "We also believe the killer is a ghost."

To her credit, Emily assimilated the information without blinking, although David could feel turmoil beginning to churn in her gut. "What makes you think this is the work of a spirit, Detective? Ghosts are not usually violent. Poltergeists, perhaps, and demons, certainly, but the ghosts of average people are usually more melancholy than dangerous. They may flick lights on or off, or perhaps take midnight strolls through your living room, but they rarely have physical interaction with the living. It's the very lack of corporeal substance that causes fear of ghosts in most people."

"Well, considering the crimes we believe this guy to be guilty of, he qualifies as a demon, for sure. We suspect that he was a serial killer in life, and has been continuing his hobby after his death, to the tune of hundreds of victims."

Emily's eyes widened and she paled, her trembling fingers touching her lips as she gasped. "*Hundreds?* Dear me. Oh those poor people…" Her clear gray eyes filled with tears.

David felt sorry for her, but there'd been no way for Hunter to soften the blow. He knew that as a psychic, Emily was extremely sensitive not only to the spirits of the dead, but to the pain of the living. The shock of hearing that hundreds of people had been brutally murdered troubled her deeply.

Hunter leaned forward, resting his forearms on his knees. The look in his eyes was direct and uncompromising. David knew Hunter was no longer nervous, not now that it was clear Emily believed him, and sympathized. "Now you understand why it's so important that we stop him. There's no reason to believe he's not going to continue doing what he does best unless we do something. Plus, there's a child involved now, a special little boy named Cooper. We believe Cooper is psychic too, Ms. Peacock. He witnessed the killer murdering the last victim. The killer, whose name we believe is Gant, has already hurt this child once. We're afraid Cooper may be killed if we don't stop Gant first."

Emily nodded. "Of course, I'll help you in any way I can, Detective Vance. That he must be stopped goes without saying."

"You don't seem to have any trouble believing that a ghost could kill the living," Hunter said. "That was the most difficult hurdle for my partner and me to get over. Why is that?"

Emily's lips curved in a small smile. "I first began sensing the dead when I was a young child, Detective. I was lucky, I suppose. The first ghost to contact me was my grandmother. I'd loved her dearly, and wasn't frightened of her in the least. Since then, I've seen and experienced too many things -- much of which was not nearly as pleasant as my grandmother's visit -- to doubt that anything is possible."

"Good. That makes this a lot easier," Hunter said. "What we need to know is how to stop Gant, hopefully before he kills again. How can I send this sorry son of a bitch to the other side, and keep him there?"

Emily stood up, and began to pace across the small space between the stacks in the center of living room. It was only a few steps, and she moved back and forth like the pendulum of a clock. Her forehead was creased with a frown. "That's a difficult question to answer, Detective. Certainly, there are ways, but none of them are foolproof. Usually, asking the ghost to leave is all it takes to do the trick. If not, sometimes a medium can reach out to the soul and entice it to go into the Light, but that would only work if the soul is lost and trying to find its way. That doesn't sound like your ghost to me."

"No, it doesn't. What other options do we have?" Hunter asked.

"Well, there are a few techniques that are commonly used." She rummaged through a few boxes, pulling out a half dozen books, and ran her forefinger along the spines. She hefted a thick volume and carried it to her chair, setting it on her lap. "What do we know of Gant from when he was alive? Was he Catholic? If he was, holy water might help."

She opened the book, flipping slowly through the pages, and continued, although she seemed to be speaking as much to herself as to them. "Sometimes cleansing a home -- what's called "smudging" -- works, but that wouldn't apply to this situation -- not if the ghost has claimed the entire city as his territory. There are reports of having good results using garlic, or blessed salt, or burning sage. Even feng shui has been known to help. Of course, like cleansing, that would be impractical," she added with a small laugh. "You couldn't very well move the skyscrapers around to achieve harmony, now could you?"

"No, I suppose not." Hunter said. "We don't know much about Gant's life. He was a sailor on the *Mary Gray*, and committed murder whenever he went ashore. He finally went on a rampage onboard the ship, killing five crew members before he was killed himself. That's about it. What about an exorcism? Would that work?"

"Thanks to movies and the media, exorcism is the most commonly known method, although the process is usually reserved for demons. It can be difficult and dangerous, particularly when attempted by someone who isn't an expert. Plus, there's no guarantee it would work."

"Tell her about the hitchhiking, Hunter," David urged.

"Oh, my partner is reminding me to tell you about a theory of his -- well, I guess it's no longer a *theory*, since he and I have both seen it work. He's discovered that ghosts can learn to leech off the emotions of the living. He calls it hitchhiking. We think Gant uses the anger in his victims to kill them."

Emily seemed to direct her smile in David's direction, and nodded. "This doesn't surprise me at all. I think your partner is very astute to have thought of it. Ghosts are attracted to strong emotions the way moths are to bright lights. I've never heard of them *sharing* in those emotions, but I can see the logic in your partner's theory."

"Tell her my name is David," he said to Hunter.

Hunter rolled his eyes. "He says to remind you his name is David."

Emily smiled again. "Yes, of course. Why do you remain on the earthly plane, David?"

Hunter, as usual, didn't bother waiting for David to answer. "We're sort of still working on that," he answered in a low murmur.

David scowled at him. "She was asking *me*, Hunter."

Hunter ignored him, much to David's chagrin. "He's a pain in the rump, but I'm used to having him around by now."

"He must have a strong attachment to you for him to resist the Light," Emily said. There was a warm look in her eyes that told David she suspected the attachment was of a romantic nature. If he could've blushed, he would have. Then again, Hunter did enough of that for the both of them. David bit back a grin as Hunter's cheeks flushed bright red.

Hunter was definitely out of his comfort zone, if the way he cleared his throat and squirmed was any indication. "Um, yeah, I guess. Anyway, we figured out that a ghost can use the emotions he hitchhikes on to physically touch things on this plane. Does that make sense to you?"

"Of course," Emily said. "There are many documented instances of poltergeists and ghosts moving objects from place to place, knocking on walls, etcetera. It's not that uncommon. What we don't know is *how* they do it, and David's theory is as good as any, I suppose. What *is* uncommon is for a ghost to intentionally hurt the living. Demonic presences are far more likely to do that than the average spirit. Are you certain about the killer's identity?"

"Yes. All the pieces fit, including the fact that he goes back to the *Mary Gray*, where he was killed."

"My experience is with finding missing persons and murder victims. I've sensed ghosts, like your partner here, but I can't hear them." She looked at Hunter. "You have been given a very rare gift, Detective Vance. I hope you can appreciate it."

To David's surprise, there was honesty in Hunter's soft reply, instead of his usual deflecting sarcasm. "I do, believe me."

"Good. Then the only thing I can suggest you do is find out more information about Gant while he was alive. Where did he come from? What sort of family life did he have? When ghosts remain in this plane, it's usually because they either don't understand that they're dead, or they have unfinished business vital enough to keep them tethered here. I'm fairly certain that this Mr. Gant is aware he's passed on, because he seems to have become quite adept at the tricks of the trade, such as touching physical matter. Therefore, I believe there's something he needs done, or undone perhaps. Once whatever it is he needs doing is finished, he'll move on."

"Do you really think it's that simple?" Hunter asked.

"Most things are. Have you ever heard of Occam's razor? The simplest explanation is usually the correct one," Emily said.

"What if he's just really into killing people? Could bloodlust be a reason for Gant to remain here?"

"Let's hope that's not the case, Detective Vance. If it is, I'm not sure how you could force him to leave without an exorcism, and even then, I'm not sure the ritual would work," Emily replied.

"It's worth a shot, Hunter," David said.

Hunter sighed, and sat back against the sofa cushions. "Somehow, I doubt asking the bastard to leave will work," he muttered. Looking at Emily, he continued, "I know we hope it doesn't come down to it, but what if all this other stuff doesn't work? What if we don't find anything on him, or even if we do, what if he refuses to go? Who do I contact about performing an exorcism?"

Emily looked away for a moment, frowning, then seemed to come to a decision. She rose and left the room, navigating the narrow corridors between stacks with an ease born of practice, and returned quickly with a piece of paper. "Promise me, Detective Hunter, that you won't use this until all other avenues have been explored. I want your word of honor."

"What is it?"

"Just promise me."

"Okay, okay. I swear we won't use it unless we absolutely have to."

Emily handed Hunter the piece of paper. There was a name and phone number written on it. "Claude Winston is a former Catholic priest. He's been…well, excommunicated from the Church because of his involvement with exorcisms. The Church frowns on them, and with good reason. I've already told you how dangerous they can be. But if all else fails, maybe he can help you. He is an expert, and has had good luck with them in the past."

Hunter stood, folding the piece of paper, and stuck it into his pocket. "Thank you, Ms. Peacock. We appreciate all of your help."

"Anytime, Detective Vance. You too, Detective Brown. I hope you can stop this lost soul before he kills again," Emily said as she showed them to the door. "Good luck."

"Thanks," Hunter said. "We're going to need it."

Chapter Sixteen

There was a major accident involving several vehicles at the entrance to the Lincoln Tunnel that had traffic at a standstill. By the time they got back into the city, the sun was setting.

They returned to Hunter's apartment in silence, armed only with the scant, new information given them by Emily and a scrap of paper that held what might very well be the name of their last hope. Hunter felt like he was trapped in a bad horror movie.

How fucking depressing was that?

Hunter kicked off his shoes and sat on the edge of the bed, unbuttoning his shirt. "Well, that was a complete waste of time, don't you think? I told you going to a psychic wasn't going to help. We don't have the luxury of time, but we managed to waste most of the fucking day."

David folded his arms, one eyebrow arching. "What do you mean? We got some valuable information, and the name of that ex-priest. Yeah, sure, Emily said to use him only as a last resort, but he must know his stuff for her to recommend him."

Hunter snorted, although there was no mirth in it. "As far as this so-called 'valuable information' goes, do you really think Gant will go away just because I ask him to nicely, or chuck a shaker of table salt at him? Not fucking likely, and as for the rest, I have news for you -- Gant isn't Linda Blair, and this isn't the set of *The Exorcist*. Some guy in a turn-around collar isn't going to solve our problems for us with a few sacrosanct words and a bottle of holy water."

"I know you're scared, Hunter. I can feel it, and it's making me jittery, too --"

Hunter growled at him, his pride dented, even though he knew David was right. "You think I'm a pussy now? I'm not afraid."

"Okay, *worried,* then. Look, I know we don't have a hell of a lot to go on here, but on the bright side, it's more than we had when you woke up this morning, right? It's worth a shot, anyway."

"*Bright side?* There's no fucking bright side to this mess, David! If I get dead, or you get blasted into the fucking Light, or wherever it is that souls are *supposed* to go when the body dies, what then? What happens to Cooper? What happens to the whole damn city?" Hunter jumped to his feet and began to pace. Contrary to what he'd told David, fear coiled in his belly like a serpent about to strike out, and he felt powerless to stop it. He'd reached his breaking point, and needed to vent or explode. He picked up a half-empty water glass he'd forgotten on the dresser the night before, and threw it across the room. The glass hit the far wall of the bedroom, shattering. Water splattered on the wall, dripping to the floorboards. "Gant will be free to go on killing like he's done for over three-quarters of a century. He'll go after Cooper, and the poor kid won't have any defense. I feel so fucking useless, David!"

"You're not useless!" David's voice rose an octave, matching the panic tightening Hunter's chest. "I know it's not much, but it's better than nothing at all, isn't it? Besides, we have no choice, Hunter. We don't have another plan. This is it. This is all we've got. We have to try."

Hunter's anger drained away, leaving black despair in its wake. He felt as if he were drowning in it, unable to take a deep breath. Never before in his entire career had he felt as impotent as he did at that moment. He'd never come up against a situation where a sharp mind or a loaded gun couldn't get him out again. He was so wrapped up in feeling miserable and useless that he almost didn't feel David's arms slip around his waist. He should have known that his emotions, although dour, were strong enough for David to hitch on.

He'd bite off his own tongue before admitted how good David's strong arms felt, and that being held went a long way toward pulling him out of the hopelessness that was eating him alive. *Besides, I don't need to. David understands. I know he does.*

"Don't do this to yourself…to us, Hunter. We can't afford a pity party right now. I feel what you're feeling and it's like I'm buried under a mountain of misery. Please, Hunter. You have to pull yourself together," David said. It sounded as if every word was being pulled out of his mouth with a pair of pliers, as if it were a colossal effort to speak, which was exactly how Hunter was feeling at the moment.

"I know, I know," Hunter said. His resolve broke and he gave in to temptation, turning in David's arms. "I can't help it. I feel so fucking worthless!" He clutched David to him, grateful beyond measure that he could actually feel David's rock-hard body in his arms, and no longer caring whether David knew it. "Give me something else to think about, David. Please? Can you? Are you…solid enough right now?" His lips brushed across David's as he spoke. They felt real, warm and soft.

"Fuck yeah," David whispered. "I'm good. More than good -- I'm fucking *ready*, Hunter."

Their kiss deepened into a long, slow exploration of each other's mouths. Hunter was besieged by the taste and texture of David's mouth, and by a myriad of subtleties and nuances he'd missed before. Hunter tasted like mint and coffee on David's tongue, which was odd considering David didn't eat or drink, and something else, something warm and earthy, and uniquely *David*. He discovered the rippled surface of the roof of David's mouth, and noticed how exquisitely hypersensitive his cheeks became when David's perpetual five o'clock shadow scraped erotically over them.

Hunter discovered a tiny chip in one of David's back molars, worn smooth by David's tongue. It intrigued Hunter because he always thought tiny imperfections like that would somehow miraculously vanish after death.

He guided David to the bed, urging him to lie down on the mattress. David's body fascinated him as well. His fingers gently explored the hard muscles moving under satiny skin, felt the texture of hair dusting David's arms and chest. They played over David's nipples, teasing each tiny nub in turn. He left David's mouth to explore his chest, nipping and licking at the nipples brought to life by his fingers.

Hunter realized he would not be satisfied until he'd tasted every inch of David's body. His tongue licked a wet path over David's flat stomach, and traced each of his sharp hipbones. He ignored David's cock for the moment – as tempting as it was – and continued to orally map each of David's legs, his thighs, his calves, his feet, and the tender skin behind each knee.

"Roll over," he whispered hoarsely. He urged David to turn over, then began to repeat the process on David's back. He licked from shoulder to shoulder, and traced each bump of David's spine with his tongue. Hunter's teeth nipped playfully at each of David's plump ass cheeks, raising pretty love bites on both.

Then, when he'd finally committed every inch of David's body to memory via his mouth and tongue, Hunter pried David's cheeks apart to expose the pink entrance he'd been dreaming about, and tasted David's most intimate flavor. He kissed David's hole, then flicked his tongue over the pebbled flesh.

David moaned and squirmed, sending a bolt of white-hot desire zinging through Hunter's balls. *David makes the sweetest noises when he'ss turned on,* Hunter thought, smiling against David's ass. *All rough and ready and sexy as hell.* He wanted to know what sounds David would make when Hunter's cock was inside him. Would David cry out or groan, curse or beg? Hunter's dick throbbed with need and dribbled precum as he formed a mental image of himself buried to the hips inside David.

"David, I want to fuck you," he whispered. "Really *fuck* you. Not blow you or jerk you off. I want inside, David."

"You're gonna make me come just talking about it, Hunter. Do it. Get in me," David answered in a husky voice. His ass lifted as if in invitation. Hunter urged David to his hands and knees and quickly took up position behind him.

Fuck! Hunter scrambled for the nightstand, tearing open the drawer and rooting around for his supplies. His hand found the bottle of lube, and he was searching for the few condoms he knew were in there somewhere when David spoke again.

"Don't need rubbers, you dickhead. I'm a ghost, remember? Come on! Fuck me already."

Hunter grinned and slammed the drawer shut, hustling back. David was right. They didn't need protection. The thought of fucking David balls deep without even the thin barrier of a condom between them brought Hunter to the razor's edge. He teetered there, trying to take back control. He had to stop and take a few deep breaths before slicking himself, fearing even the touch of his own hand on his cock would send him over.

"What are you waiting for?" David asked brusquely. He glared over his shoulder at Hunter with lust-darkened eyes.

"Give me a minute, will ya?" Hunter breathed. He rubbed a hand over David's ass. "Man, that's pretty. Such a fucking hot ass, David. Gonna fuck you until you scream."

"Do it then," David whispered. His voice was low and rumbling. "Now. I want to feel you inside me."

"Now, yeah. Now." Hunter squeezed a dollop of lube over the David's crack, using his finger to work it into David's hole. He slipped a finger inside David, all the way to the knuckle. "Feel that? My finger, inside you."

David moaned, his ass hitching. "Feels good, Hunter."

"Gonna feel better. My cock in you next."

"Yeah. Give it. Want your cock. Now."

"Now," Hunter repeated. He pulled his finger away and pushed the head of his cock against David's asshole. Go slow, he ordered himself. *Slowly, don't want to hurt him. He's never done this before.* Hunter took his time, sliding in inch by torturous inch, pushing his way past clenching muscle until at last he was fully seated.

Inside David.

In him.

Hunter let out a long breath between clenched teeth, holding his body rigid, not wanting to move, yet desperate to ram himself in and out, to fuck David raw.

David moaned, and lowered his head to rest on his forearms. "Fuck! Hunter…you're in me."

"I know."

"Feels…good. Hurts, but good. Full, you know?"

"Yeah, I know. Gonna move now. Gonna fuck you."

He tilted his hips, angling to find David's sweet spot. He knew he hit it when David groaned loudly.

"Fuck, Hunter! More. Do that more!"

Hunter was happy to oblige. He set a hard pace, the sound of flesh slapping flesh filling his ears with the music of sex.

David slid to his belly, and Hunter followed along, still pounding into David's ass. "Gonna come, David. Gonna come inside you."

"Do it! Want to feel it!"

"What do you want to feel? Tell me," Hunter demanded. He was breathing hard, feeling his balls swell with his impending climax. The words would send him over, he knew.

"Want to feel your cum. Fill me up. All the way up, Hunter!"

Hunter howled as he came, his hips pumping his cock into David's ass like pistons. His orgasm was so powerful it bordered on pain, and stars danced briefly behind his tightly closed eyelids.

His eyes were still half-hooded and his belly still clenching with the aftershocks of his climax when he roughly rolled David over and took David's cock in his mouth. He had given David his essence, and wanted David's in return. Tit for tat, he thought wildly as he sucked hard on David's prick.

David's hands held Hunter's head, and his hips lifted to feed Hunter his cock. Hunter felt a few drops of bitter salt just before David came. He refused to let David pull away, drinking every last drop David had to offer, then licking David's cock clean.

He flopped back on the bed next to David with a happy, satisfied grin on his face. Never had sex been as intense, as soul-scorching as it had with David. Somewhere deep inside, Hunter knew he would never find it with anyone else. Only David could make him feel so totally connected, so completely satisfied.

Only David.

He realized something else in that moment, as he lay panting for breath next to the man he loved more than his own life: his fear was gone. He was no longer afraid to face Gant, no longer felt helpless. He would do whatever it took to rid the world of Gant, and keep David by his side.

* * * * *

"We're going to do this," David whispered. He lay on his side, watching Hunter's face. "We're going to make it." He tried to smooth hair away from Hunter's forehead, but his fingers passed through the strands. Hunter was sleeping, having dropped off moments after they'd finished making love, and his unconscious state precluded David's hitchhiking.

That's what it was this time, he decided. It had been making love. It wasn't the unbridled, feral sex they'd had before when anger had been the springboard to their physical connection. It had been great then, phenomenal even, but this time even more memorable, and even more intense. This time it had been sweet between them, and tender, and then hot and hard and…complete. Yeah, that was a good word. Complete. Hunter made him feel whole, alive again. He smirked, knowing that Hunter would laugh and think David's thoughts were too girly, but it was the truth. David knew he'd treasure the memory no matter what the future held for him, even though he knew it was going to make his decision to leave Hunter all the more difficult.

As much as he would like to ignore it, David had felt time in a new way since leaving Emily Peacock's house. It felt heavy, ponderous, weighing down on his shoulders, threatening to squash him flat. In his mind, a small, wicked voice whispered it was because he knew he'd be saying good-bye to Hunter soon. They would go after Gant and succeed (they *had* to succeed; David refused to even consider the alternative), and then David would be left with only one last thing to do -- leave. David would have to force himself to depart the mortal plane so that Hunter could have some semblance of a normal life.

This is what hell is like. David rolled to his back and stared at the ceiling. *It's not roasting in fire or freezing in ice like the old priest in my parish used to tell us when I was a kid. Hell is facing an eternity of being without the one you love.*

If he wasn't so certain that Hunter was emitting no emotions for him to use to hitchhike, David would swear he felt miserably depressed.

Chapter Seventeen

"Are you ready for this?" David asked. They were standing on the wharf, facing the black ship, the *Mary Gray*. Their plan was simple, although far from foolproof. David would use his psychic connection to find Gant, and hopefully lure Gant to where Hunter waited. Then Hunter would take Gant out.

They hoped.

Hunter looked down at the two objects he held in his hand. The ziplock baggie of salt, hastily blessed by a priest at a church near Hunter's apartment, and a squeeze bottle of holy water pinched from the font at the same church seemed like ludicrous weapons. Not for the first time, he wished his gun would be effective. He felt naked knowing that drawing it would offer him and David no protection.

The old priest at the neighborhood church, to his credit, hadn't asked why Hunter wanted him to bless a plastic baggie full of table salt. He'd simply uttered a prayer, his hand moving quickly in the Sign of the Cross in the air over the baggie.

Hunter got the feeling the priest thought Hunter was slightly off his rocker -- not that Hunter blamed the poor old guy. Maybe it was the urgency in Hunter's gruff voice when he asked the priest to sanctify the salt that made the priest uneasy. After all, how often could it be that a detective for the great City of New York called upon aged priests to do emergency salt blessings? Then again, perhaps it was more common than Hunter realized. In any case, the priest asked no questions, but made the Sign of the Cross over the proffered bag. He left quickly, almost running through the church into the sacristy, his black cassock flapping around his skinny ankles, leaving Hunter standing alone in the vestibule holding his blessed plastic baggie of Morton's Iodized table salt. It was just as well. Hunter wasn't in the mood for lengthy explanations anyway. He took advantage of the opportunity to pilfer a squeeze bottle full of holy water from one of the fonts at the church's entrance.

"Tell me the truth, David. Do you *really* think this is going to work?" Hunter asked, holding up the baggie and bottle.

"Of course. Don't you?" David looked confident and not the least bit nervous, but Hunter got the feeling his coolness was a sham. David had to be feeling Hunter's unease. Hunter grudgingly gave him credit for hiding it so well.

"Me? I think we'd have a better chance building igloos in hell." Hunter said truthfully, as he slipped both items into his pockets. He glanced at David. "You know, I'm not sure I trust this new, optimistic you."

"Bite me."

"Nah. It would be like chewing on a mouthful of air. Not exactly impressive," Hunter replied, shooting for a cheekiness he didn't feel. He took a deep breath and straightened his spine. "Okay, I'm ready. Let's do this thing."

Their banter made everything seem almost normal, although Hunter knew it was only a paper-thin façade. David always felt what Hunter was feeling, which, at the moment, was somewhere in the realm of scared shitless. Still, it brought them both back into the arena of the familiar, at least for a few minutes.

David nodded. "I'm going to check Gant's cabin aboard the ship first. If he's not there, I'll connect to his head again and see if I can find him. Either way, I'll try to lure him out here to you." He started to fade away, but turned back. "Hunter, listen…if things don't work out the way we planned today --"

Hunter shook his head. He knew what David was going to say, but didn't want to talk about anything even vaguely connected to their feelings for each other. His hold on his nerves was tenuous at best; being distracted by sharing intimacies would only serve to distract him, and weaken his grip. Not to mention make him as uncomfortable as all get out. Pillow talk belonged on the fucking pillows, not during the line of duty. "Man up. We'll be okay. Go get him."

David, as stubborn in death as he ever was in life, refused to budge. Damn him.

"No, I need to tell you again, in case I don't get the chance later."

"David, you're not going anywhere…"

"I love you, Hunter," David said, cutting Hunter off and turning away again. "I just needed to say it again." He disappeared without waiting for a reply, and didn't return.

Hunter stared at the spot David had vacated, and felt the innocuous objects in his pocket, trying to get his concentration back. It was no use. He couldn't pretend he was just doing his job anymore. Nothing about this case bore any resemblance whatsoever to anything he'd ever done before, and now David had just reminded him that he was fighting for something even more monumental than justice.

But hey, no pressure, right?

Feeling helpless, nervous, and at the same time, determined, Hunter grit his teeth and waited.

* * * * *

David faded into the nothingness of space, negotiating a small enough wrinkle to put him inside the ship's cabin once belonging to Gant.

Pretending to be confident in front of Hunter had been difficult. What he really wanted to do was grab Hunter and run, to put as much distance between them and Gant as possible. Hawaii would be good. Australia, maybe. Antarctica wasn't beyond the scope of possibility. Fuck going into the Light or the void or whatever lay beyond the veil. He would find a nice, safe hidey-hole with Hunter and stay put. Love Hunter. Fuck him until both he and Hunter forgot all about New York and serial killers.

It was a pipe dream. They couldn't run, and he knew it. They had to face Gant and stop him, if for no other reason than to make sure Cooper would be safe. But that didn't make it any easier on either of them. David kept picking up on Hunter's anxiety, and it made David feel as jumpy as a whore in church.

At least he'd finally summoned up the nerve to say the words that'd been on his mind for years. I love you. Three simple words that had stuck in his craw like a fishbone while he'd been alive, and had been just as difficult to dislodge after he was dead. Now it seemed he couldn't *stop* saying them. He wondered if Hunter thought he was a pussy for wanting to say them so often. Real men didn't discuss their feelings, right? The closest he'd ever gotten when alive and on the force was some grunting and chest-bumping, maybe a little ass-swatting in the locker room.

He supposed he would've felt better if Hunter had said the words back to him again. Not that he'd given Hunter the chance. No, he'd disappeared like the fucking Cheshire Cat before Hunter could do more than blink.

God, he was such a fucking coward sometimes.

All right, enough of the girly emotional shit, before you start rolling curlers in your hair and painting your fucking toenails. Concentrate! You have to have your wits about you if you're going back into that septic tank Gant calls a mind. He pushed aside his thoughts of Hunter and concentrated on Gant.

Gant's psychic stench permeated the room. He's been here recently, David thought, wrinkling his nose. *He must've come back sometime after I was here and spoke with Abel.*

As if merely thinking the man's name had summoned him like a genie from the proverbial bottle, Abel Smith appeared at David's elbow. "Ain't caught him yet, have ye? That scoundrel is as slippery as a seal in a barrel o' butter."

"Have you seen him, Abel?" David asked. "It's important to tell me if you have. I think we may have found a way to get rid of him once and for all."

"A-yup, but I didn't have to *see* him to know he was here," Abel said. "Bastard sends a cold wave through the whole o' the ship when he arrives. Poor girl rocks in her moorings like a frightened child, she does." He patted the wall next to him, as if to reassure the ship of his presence. Neither of them commented on the way his fingers slid through the wall.

"When was he here last?"

"Not twelve hours ago, by me reckoning. You say ye have a plan? Best to get on with it then, and be quick about it. He's a-going to kill again. Mark me words. I can feel it in me bones."

David refrained from mentioning that Abel didn't *have* any bones, no more than David did. He figured Abel knew Gant better than anyone else, having known Gant in life as well as all the years following, and if he said Gant was gearing up for another murder, then David believed him.

God, he didn't want to do this. He hadn't touched Gant's mind since the first time because he dreaded the images he knew were stored in Gant's head. Every murder Gant had committed played on the screen of his mind like some long-running horror movie fest. David came to the ship in hopes of finding Gant so he could avoid being forced into a front row seat at Gant's private slasher marathon.

Now, however, David was out of luck, options, and time.

Closing his eyes, David reached out with his mind and found the connection he held with Gant.

Reptilian coldness spiked through David's entire being as he found and caught hold of Gant's psyche, accompanied by tumbling images of gore, and feelings of hate so potent they rattled David to his core. Gant, he realized, hated everyone and everything equally and without prejudice.

In Gant's mind, there was no good at all in the world, nothing worth treasuring, nothing redeeming. Everything must be destroyed, every life snuffed out if Gant was to attain some measure of peace. Gant's hatred had poisoned him from the inside out.

Why did Gant hate so fiercely? Had he been born with the wires already crossed in his brain, or did something happen along the way to warp him? If it was the latter, and David could find out what it was, the information might prove useful to himself and Hunter in their confrontation with Gant. It was worth taking a moment -- and braving the cesspool of Gant's memories -- to find out.

Holding his fictional breath, David forced himself to dive deeper through Gant's recollections, trying not to look too hard at the scenes of murder and mayhem that made up the bulk of Gant's mnemonic scrapbook.

But dear God, there are so many! Face after face flashed through David's mind, each a study in terror. Decade after decade, each month stained with blood, flipped before David's eyes like some sort of twisted Marquis de Sade pinup calendar.

A nurse in the nineties, killed with a nail-studded two-by-four. A sailor on shore leave in the eighties, murdered with a crowbar. A stockbroker in the seventies, his life snuffed out by the sharp, jagged end of a broken chair leg. A hippie in the sixties died with flowers in her hair and a screwdriver driven deep into her chest, blood staining her white granny dress crimson. There was a street tough with a black leather jacket, and a DA in the fifties, who was beaten to death with the side view mirror torn from his own motorcycle. In the forties, there was a veteran returning from World War II who never made it home, strangled by Gant with a length of chain. And more. So very many more.

Each victim had been feeling angry at the time. As David delved deeper, he realized that the level of anger in each victim dropped significantly. He felt little satisfaction in the knowledge that he'd been correct in his assumption that as time went on, Gant needed less and less emotional anger to hitchhike on in order to work up a killing rage. It only made the need to stop Gant that much more imperative. At this rate, David figured Gant would only need to find someone mildly irritated in order to kill.

The stream of dead faces slowed to a trickle, and finally stopped. David found himself surrounded by indistinct images cloaked in darkness, and realized he was in the subbasement of Gant's mind. This was where Gant stored his darkest memories, the ones so vile and painful to him that he tried to bury them under the sea of blood from his victims.

David paused, unsure if he wanted to rip the shrouds from Gant's buried memories, not certain he wanted to see what lay there. Only the thought of Hunter and Cooper's safety enabled him to move forward. Sucking in and holding a breath that didn't really exist, David focused on the nearest memory within reach.

He found himself in a crib, looking out between the slats through the eyes of a boy no more than one or two years old. David knew instinctively that the boy was Gant.

There were two adults in the room, a man and a woman, and they were arguing. Gant couldn't understand why mama and dada were so angry. The man picked Gant up and shook him so violently his small baby teeth clacked together, chipping two of them. David could taste the metallic tang of blood that filled Gant's mouth.

David shook the memory off, and reluctantly moved to the next.

In this one, a woman held Gant, now three or four years old, firmly by one arm. A stinging slap left Gant's ears ringing. David doesn't know why the woman, whom David presumes to be Gant's mother, is angry with him. Neither, David realizes, does Gant.

Gant is older yet in the next memory, perhaps seven or eight, and in the kitchen. He is cowering in a corner next to the ice box, his thin arms crooked over his head trying to protect himself from the vicious blows his mother rains down upon him. Nearby, a shattered mug lay in a spill of milk on the floor.

David moves on, needing to know the extent of Gant's cruel childhood. The next memory he uncovers is of Gant's father screaming his name, furious over something Gant has done. A broom stands in a corner of the room, a handy weapon for the man to use to beat the defenseless child.

Finally, David finds a memory of a teenaged Gant poised on the brink of manhood, staring into a mirror at the scars his parents' abuse has left on his face. They intersect his skin like the fine white strands of a spider's web, ghostly precursors to the burns Gant would one day sustain on his face. Twin trails of small, round scars spot his forearms, burned into his flesh by the glowing red tips of his father's cigarettes. Without needing to see them, David knows Gant has suffered other scars, deeper and more painful, still raw, never healing, no matter how much time has passed. For the first time, David notices that the fear in Gant's eyes has been replaced by hate and madness.

David felt a prick of unease, like ghostly fingers jabbing at his brain, but shruggged it off as his imagination. He continued to force himself to look at Gant's memories, each more horrific than the one before, but soon severed the connection between them. The last memory he visited was one too many; he'd seen enough.

He'd found the ammunition he'd come to get. Instead of leaving to find Gant, he decided to go back to Hunter and fill Hunter in one what he'd found. It might give them the edge they needed when they finally confronted Gant.

He hoped.

Chapter Eighteen

David flinched as a stream of water hit him directly between the eyes -- or would have, had he been corporeal. Even so, it was still disconcerting to have a blast of water shoot straight through your head. "Hunter, knock it off! It's me."

"Shit," Hunter spat. He held a toy water pistol in his hand. He looked embarrassed as he quickly shoved the plastic gun back inside his pocket. "I thought you were Gant. Where is he?"

"First of all, fear isn't what's going to let Gant attack. You have to be angry, Hunter, not afraid. Second, what the fuck are you going to do? Drown him?"

"It's the holy water. I put it in the water pistol," Hunter said. "Figured the gun would make it easier to nail him. Plus, it makes me feel better to have a gun in my hand, even if it's only a dime store kiddie toy. Where the hell did you go?"

"Inside Gant's head. The dude is one twisted individual, Hunter. I don't know if he was born a sociopath, but he became one before he hit his teens. He had no conscience, and was unable to love anyone but himself. He was abused as a kid, badly, and the cycle repeated itself as he grew older and became an abuser himself. His parents warped him, poisoned him, and the abuse contributed to his insanity."

"How does knowing this help us?"

"He murdered both his parents, Hunter. They were his first victims. He buried them beneath the floorboards of their house. I think he's been killing them ever since, over and over again, seeing them in every victim he's murdered. After he died, he missed being angry, missed the hatred that was a part of him for so long, and the release murdering gave him. He hungers for it, Hunter. Needs it like an addict needs meth."

Hunter swore under his breath. "And again, how does this information help us stop Gant?"

"His parents' house is still here, Hunter. It's now a multifamily home in Flushing. He goes there every so often, drawn by his past, I guess. After he killed his parents, he hired onto the *Mary Gray*, so the house would've stood vacant for a good, long while before the city would've claimed it for taxes, and resold it. There's a possibility that the bodies were never found."

"You think unearthing his folks' remains will stop him?" Hunter asked.

"I think we should check it out. If the bodies are still there, confronting him on the site about their murders might unsettle him, and give us an edge."

"Or piss him off."

"I hope so, since that's the only way for us to get rid of him, but that'll only happen if *you're* angry. He can't work up anger on his own, and it's the only way you'll be able to bridge the gap between the living and the dead and take him out. Look, it's worth a shot, right? We can use every advantage we can get, Hunter. Let's face it…right now all we have is a kid's water gun and a handful of table salt. That's not exactly a full arsenal, now is it?"

Hunter sighed, but nodded his head. "I suppose you're right. I hate putting this off another minute, though, David. I want him gone *now*. I want things to go back to the way they used to be."

David looked away. Nothing was going to be the way it was before. He was leaving after they got rid of Gant, going into the Great Fucking White Light, but there was no sense in telling Hunter about his plans now. Hunter would only try to talk him out of it, and the last thing he needed was to be any more distracted than he already was. "I plucked the location of Gant's parents' house from his head. It's in Flushing, on Farrington Street. Let's roll."

* * * * *

Gant's family home was a two-story structure, and luckily for them (they hadn't taken the time to try to get a search warrant because, after all, what judge would give them one based on evidence collected by a ghost?), it was empty. A FOR SALE sign sat crookedly on the tiny front lawn, the realtor's name and phone number nearly obliterated by graffiti.

The house was a definite handyman special. The same graffiti decorating the FOR SALE sign was spray painted in a multitude of colors across the front of the house. A chain link fence surrounded the miniscule front yard, but the grass within it was sparse and brown. The picture window on the first floor had a long, jagged crack running across it, and several other, smaller windows were boarded up. Hunter could see that more shingles were missing from the roof than were still attached to it. The tiny cement stoop was dirty, and crumbling.

A quick look showed that a padlock had been installed on the front door, and there was no way for them to get inside without cutting it. That smacked too much of breaking and entering to suit Hunter. They had probable cause as far as he was concerned, but he wouldn't want to have to explain why to the captain back at headquarters. Their luck improved when they walked around the side of the house to the backyard, and found the back door wide open. The lock had been broken off completely, and the doorknob removed.

One corner of Hunter's mouth lifted in a wry grin. "Huh. Looks like someone broke in," he said. "That's enough probable cause for the cap to understand us entering without a warrant, right?"

"You betcha," David agreed. He gestured grandly toward the door. "After you."

Hunter and David stepped inside. One of the neighborhood gangs must've been using the downstairs apartment as a party house for some time. The walls were sprayed with graffiti, and the floor littered with empty booze bottles, drug paraphernalia, and used condoms. The air was stale and reeked of weed.

There was no furniture in the apartment to speak of, aside from a single, slat-backed rocking chair, a couple of rusted metal folding chairs, and an old, ratty sofa the gang members probably found in the trash somewhere and dragged inside.

"Do you have any idea where the bodies might be, if they're still here?" Hunter asked David. He carried a crowbar, taken from the trunk of his car.

"Yeah. According to the memory I saw in Gant's head, they're under the floorboards in the master bedroom closet."

They made their way into the master bedroom, differentiated from the other two bedrooms only by its slightly larger size. There was no private bath, and the only furniture was a filthy, bare mattress on the floor. The closet door hung partway off its hinges, leaning at an awkward angle against the wall.

Hunter poked his head inside the closet took a sniff. Of course, there was no smell other than mustiness and the ghost of mothballs. The bodies -- if they were still there -- would be far too old for decomposition to be an issue.

Kneeling on the floor of the closet, he worked his fingers under the edge of the threadbare carpet covering the floor, and yanked hard. The rug and padding came up with a puff of dust, revealing the stained and worn hardwood flooring underneath.

He slid one end of the crowbar between the slats, ready to pry up the first of the floorboards, when a shrill voice froze him in place.

"What are you doing? Harry? What's he doing to our floor?"

A deeper voice followed the first. "Hey, you two…get out of there. You're trespassing. Damaging private property. I'll set the law on you."

Hunter looked up. Two people stood behind David, a man and a woman. They were only semitransparent -- he could see right through them to the bedroom window on the far side of the room. He realized with a start that they were both dead. He'd never seen another ghost before, at least not to his knowledge.

Well, there's a first time for everything. Maybe my new relationship with David has done something to me. Swell. Just what I need. Something told him he was right. "Who the fuck are these two?" he asked David.

"Beats me," David replied. He did a double take. "You can see them?"

"Yeah. Lucky me, huh?"

"You can hear them too?"

"Loud and clear."

"Huh. Well, what do you know?" David looked at the ghosts and rephrased Hunter's question. "Who are you?"

"If you must know, I'm Harold Gant, and this is my wife, Esther. This is our house. You have no business here."

David gave a low whistle, and looked at Hunter. "I never thought they'd still be here. Murder victims usually hightail it away from the scene as soon as possible. I never really gave any thought as to whether their ghosts would still be in the house, Hunter."

"Do you think Gant knows about them?" Hunter eyed Gant's parents. His father was tall and lean, with sharp features. Gant's mother looked nearly as stringy as her husband, with a narrow face and thin lips. Neither one looked particularly friendly.

Quite frankly, Hunter didn't know how to feel about the two ghosts. They'd been horrible people in life, true slime for abusing their son, but did that justify their murders? He found he couldn't feel sorry for them. Child abusers rated the same as maggots in Hunter's book.

But he was still a cop, and vigilante justice didn't sit well with him. He knew the courts in the nineteen twenties and thirties would've turned a blind eye to domestic violence, considering it a "family affair," and would most likely have done nothing to stop Gant's parents from abusing their child, but that didn't justify Gant killing them, did it? Even if it did, it certainly didn't excuse Gant's murder of innocent people over the following decades.

"I didn't see anything in his memories, but I'm willing to book that he does. It could be the reason he keeps killing -- he's still trying to get rid of them."

"I told those delinquents not to come in here either," Harold said. "Look at what they did to the walls in the parlor! They've ruined our house."

"Somebody should do something about those children, running wild like they do. They're savages," Esther added.

"Now here you two are, doing more damage to my property. I won't have it, do you hear? I'll get the law on you." Although the words were angry, Harold's voice remained a dull monotone. Evidently, Gant's parents hadn't learned how to hitchhike, not that Hunter was feeling any emotion at the moment other than total disgust.

"Well, you're in luck then, because I *am* the law," Hunter said. He slipped his badge out of his pocket and flashed it at the ghosts.

Their reaction wasn't what he'd expected. Both curled their lips, and backed away as if they were vampires and he held a stake fashioned from the One True Cross. He figured it was because they hadn't been the most upright citizens while alive.

"Does your son know you're here?" David asked them.

Esther began wailing, a thin, eerie sound that sounded as transparent as she was. Without emotions to back it, her cry was only a weak attempt at sympathy. Hunter rolled his eyes at her.

"The boy? Useless. Worthless," Harold spat. "He came home drunk! I told him I wouldn't put up with the devil's drink in my home! I backhanded him a good one. Told him I'd beat the devil out of him. I tried, too. Took after him with my belt, but I only got a few good wallops in before... Do you know what that Satan-spawn did? He picked up Mother's cleaver and..." His voice trailed off and he looked away, as if he'd just remembered something horrible and couldn't bear to continue.

He probably had -- he'd remembered his own murder at the hands of his son.

Hunter frowned, then turned away, determined to ignore them both. He found it hard to feel pity for a pair of monsters who'd abused their child. Sick bastards, he thought, as he knelt down again and returned to his original task -- prying loose the closet floorboards. He pulled up enough wood to clear a foot-wide hole. Taking a penlight from his pocket, he directed the thin beam into the opening. The beam illuminated dust, and a dull gray object, covered with over fifty years of filth and mold.

No matter how dirty, there was no mistaking it for what it was -- a skull. The two empty eye sockets seemed to stare back at him.

Hunter didn't know if the skull once belonged to Harold or to Esther, and quickly decided it didn't matter. All that did was that David had been right -- the bones were still here, and evidently, so were the ghosts. The combination of the two might be what kept Gant tethered to the mortal plane, continuing his murderous rampage. Would facing Gant in their presence be enough to distract Gant and give Hunter an edge over him?

He looked up, meeting David's eyes, and gave a quick, sharp nod. "You were right. The bones are here. Can you get Gant to come?"

"I'm right here, you idiot," Harold said. "Are you blind as well as deaf? I said to get out! Get out!"

They both ignored Harold.

"I can try," David said. "Are you sure you're ready?"

"As I can be," Hunter replied. He stood up, leaned the crowbar against the wall, and clapped the dust from his hands.

"Um, you might want to stick that back inside the car," David said, pointing to the crowbar. "I don't think it's a good idea to leave anything lying around that Gant can use as a weapon."

"Good point," Hunter said. He picked up the crowbar, and ran outside, locking it in the trunk of his car. When he returned, the elder Gants were still hovering around David, haranguing him about the damage to the closet floor. Seemed they'd forgotten all about their son and their murders at his hands already. "David? Are you ready?"

"Yeah. Let's do this thing," David replied, jerking his thumb toward the Gants. "Anything to get away from these two. They're driving me crazy. If they weren't already dead, I think I might just kill them myself."

Hunter dug out the water pistol full of holy water, and the baggie of salt, holding them at the ready. He exchanged a meaningful look with David. Win or lose, it had come down to this moment. "Go for it," he said, and waited for David to disappear, leaving him alone with the elder Gants.

As it turned out, David didn't need to go very far. In fact, he didn't need to go anywhere at all.

Chapter Nineteen

Gant popped into view, standing between his parents and David and Hunter. Harold backpedaled, and Esther shrieked, and although her scream was monotonic and lifeless, it nonetheless added to the waves of agitation David was picking up from Hunter.

David automatically stepped in front of Hunter, as if to shield him. In a small part of his mind, he realized old habits died hard. He'd always tried to shield Hunter in life too. The practice was what had finally gotten David killed.

"Who the fuck…is that him? Is it Gant?" Hunter demanded. The agitation deepened into anger. "Get out of my way, David!"

David ignored him. Gant used anger to kill, and right now, Hunter was exuding it like dime store cologne. He knew he needed to give Hunter a clear shot at Gant, but couldn't seem to force himself to move. He'd protected Hunter too many times in the past to step aside now.

David's mind raced, trying to figure out how Gant had found them. This wasn't how they'd planned it. How did Gant manage it? Was it only coincidence that brought Gant to his parents' home while David and Hunter were still there? Somehow, he doubted it. He had a disturbing feeling he was missing something, something important.

A heartbeat later, Gant proved David right.

Gant's mouth stretched in a macabre parody of a grin. The skin on his face seemed to stretch tight, making his head look skull-like, cadaverous, made even more frightening by the horrid burns covering most it. Gant pointed a long, bony finger at David. "Did you think I wouldn't notice you scuttling around inside my head, picking at my brain? Pick, pick, pick, like a rat nibbling cheese. Stupid, stupid. I *knew* you were there the whole time. I *felt* you."

David was completely shocked by what Gant had revealed. *Gant knew I was in his head!* David had been so sure Gant was unaware. He'd naïvely assumed the pathway between his mind and Gant's had been one way only, and now he got the distinct feeling he was going to pay for his arrogance. Had Gant been picking David's brain while David prowled the blood-soaked hallways in Gant's mind? Was that what the uneasy feeling had been that David remembered? *If I was wrong about that much, what other mistakes did I make?*

Esther continued to shriek, her undulating wail filling the room. Gant turned on his mother with a snarl. "Shut up, bitch!"

David was so absorbed by his disturbing thoughts and their possible ramifications that he almost missed Hunter dodging around him. He caught the movement out of the corner of his eye as Hunter took advantage of Gant's momentary distraction, drew his gun and fired at Gant.

It took David a moment to realize there'd been no shots fired; instead, a stream of water zipped past him, hitting Gant squarely in the face. The holy water, he thought absently, even as he stuck an arm out and tried to push Hunter behind him again. He wasn't concentrating, and his arm passed right through Hunter like a knife through air.

"Die, you fucker! Why won't you die?" Hunter screamed. Hunter's fury was palpable; David felt it throbbing inside him as he inadvertently hitched on it. He reached out again, and managed to push Hunter backward a step or two.

Gant gasped and staggered when the water hit him. To David's surprise, the water didn't pass through Gant as it had David. It dripped over Gant's forehead and cheeks, and seemed to sizzle on his ghostly skin like water on a hot frying pan. "Oh, you wicked bastards! No fair, no fair! I'll get even. There's more than one way to skin a cat, and I know where the little kitty is that you two are protecting. You'll be sorry. You wait and see!" Gant roared, before disappearing in the blink of an eye.

"Where'd he go?" Hunter demanded. "David, did it work? Could it be that easy? Is he gone for good?"

"Get even? What does he know that I don't?" David said, more to himself than to Hunter. His mind worked rapidly, and then it came to him. If he were still alive, David knew the revelation would've felt like a punch to the gut. "Oh shit…oh fuck!" He turned to Hunter. "No, it didn't work, Hunter. All we did was piss him off. Gant left this house, not the mortal plane, but I know where he's going. Get in the truck and drive over to St. Luke's as fast as you can. He's going after Cooper."

David popped out of the room before Hunter could ask any questions. There was no time. He had to get to Cooper before Gant hurt the boy.

* * * * *

Never before, at least not since the earliest days when David had just been learning how to fold distance, did he feel as clumsy and slow at maneuvering through the fluff of space. He supposed it was panic, or what passed as dread for ghosts, remnants of the anger he'd hitched from Hunter, that had him feeling distraught and distracted. He popped into the hallway on the wrong floor of the hospital. He was confused for a moment; the nurse's desk wasn't where it should be, and the room numbers were wrong. It took him precious seconds to get his bearings, to figure out where he was, slip back into space and out again on the correct floor, in Cooper's room.

To his eternal dismay, the delay cost dearly.

Emma Weils lay face down on the floor next to Cooper's bed, a crimson puddle slowly spreading out from under her head. A glint of metal in Gant's hand gave the cause. In the few seconds he'd been alone in the room before David arrived, Gant had stabbed her in the throat with a butter knife, probably one snatched from Cooper's dinner tray.

Cooper lay on the bed, motionless. For a long, terrifying moment, David thought Gant had killed him too, but then he noticed Cooper's narrow chest slowly rising and falling under the thin, white sheet. As David watched, he saw the wraithlike form of Cooper's astral-self rise from the boy's body. A wave of grief and terror washed over him as he picked up on Cooper's emotions. Chances were good Cooper had seen Gant stab his mother, and fainted.

A piercing scream and the clatter of dishes hitting the linoleum floor came from behind David. He turned, and saw an orderly, the large, rolling lunch tray cart behind her, staring at Emma's body. Another scream followed closely on the heels of the first, and David could hear other voices calling out, and feet running in the direction of the room. The murder had been discovered. He knew that in a very short time, the room would be crawling first with hospital staff, and then with the police.

David swore. He didn't need any more distractions, or the problems heightened emotions from the staff would bring. Gant could easily use them to hurt Cooper. For now, Gant was powerless since the only emotion in the room was the fear and grief coming from Cooper.

Emma's ghost, pale and ethereal, hovered near Cooper's bed. Her face held the blank, confused expression of the newly dead as she looked from her son to her body and back again. David barely paid her any mind; his attention was focused on the small form lying in bed, and Gant's tall, thin specter hovering close by.

"Mama!" Astral-Cooper's plaintive cry filled the room. His eyes were wide with terror, fixed on the ghostly form of his mother. They reached out for each other, but Emma, so new to death and still helpless, couldn't make physical contact with him. His tiny hands passed through hers.

"Get away from him," David said to Gant, taking a step forward. "He's nothing to you."

"True enough," Gant replied, flashing David a smile that would've made David's skin crawl had he been alive. "But he means a great deal to you. I saw it in your head."

"Leave him alone, Gant. So help me, I'll --"

"You'll do what? You can't do anything to me. *I* decide who lives or dies. *Me*, not you!" Gant hissed. "What was it your friend sprayed on me back in my house? It burned! I haven't felt pain in so long…I *liked* it." His mouth stretched in a death's-head grin.

"You're one fucked-up bastard, Gant. Get away from Cooper!"

David took another step toward the bed, but Gant was faster. Wrapping an arm around astral-Cooper, Gant disappeared, taking astral-Cooper with him. Cooper's physical self remained unmoving on the bed. Emma Weils' ghost tried to touch him once more, but of course, she failed.

"My baby. Help him." Emma's voice was even and emotionless, a pale imitation of what she'd been in life, but David knew her love for Cooper was strong enough to keep her tethered to the hospital room until astral-Cooper was found and returned.

Cursing again, David sent Emma Weils' ghost a pitying look. "We'll get Cooper back, Emma. I promise. Stay here. At the very least, you can say good-bye to him when this is over."

He popped out of the room and navigated space into the front seat of Hunter's car.

* * * * *

Hunter barked an epithet, and the car swerved sharply to the right when David appeared in the passenger seat. David barely noticed. "You're not going to like this," he said. There was simply no way to soften the news. It would be best to get it over with quickly, like ripping off a Band-Aid. "Gant killed Emma Weils, Hunter. Right in front of Cooper."

Brakes squealed and horns blared as Hunter jammed his foot down on the pedal, bringing the car to a screeching halt in the middle of traffic. "What? Oh fuck, no! How? How did the bastard work up enough juice to do it?"

"I'm sorry. It's true. I don't know exactly how he managed it. Either Emma was angry about something, or someone else nearby was," David said. It was purely supposition, but seemed the most reasonable explanation. "Gant used the anger to kill her. He stabbed her in the throat with a butter knife. There's more too. Cooper must've fainted, because astral-Cooper came out just as I got there. Gant disappeared, and he took astral-Cooper with him. The hospital was just discovering the body when I left. You're going to get called to the scene, Hunter."

"Fuck that. I won't answer my phone. The murder is going to have to wait. We have to find Cooper before Gant finds a way to kill him too."

David nodded. He expected no less. Hunter would know Emma was beyond their help, but Cooper was not. "I think he may have taken Cooper back to the *Mary Gray*. It seems the most likely place. Oh, one more thing. Gant said the holy water *burned* him, Hunter. Said he liked it, the sick fuck. I don't know if he was lying."

"Good. Maybe he was telling the truth. Maybe we really *can* send this bastard to hell. Well, what are you still doing here? Go! Keep that bastard away from Cooper until I can get there. I think the time for playing around with salt and water pistols is over. I'm not taking any more chances with this. I'm going to get the priest."

David didn't have to be told twice.

Chapter Twenty

Hunter sped toward the address written on the small card given him by Emily Peacock. It was on West Fifty-sixth Street, not far from the pier where the *Mary Gray* was anchored. He ignored traffic signals when possible, dodged around vehicles, and took corners on two wheels, screeching to a halt in front of the reddish-brown building. He double-parked, jumped out of the car and took the steps on the stoop two at a time.

Apartment 3B was listed as the one belonging to Claude Winston, former Catholic priest and expert in exorcisms. He rang the bell, shifting his weight from foot to foot as he waited for an answer, praying Winston was at home.

Luck, for once, was on his side. A man's voice, tinny and distorted, sounded from the intercom box on the side of the front door. "Who is it?"

"My name is Detective Hunter Vance. I need to speak to you for a moment."

"About what?"

"Please, Father…er, Mr. Winston, it's very important," Hunter said. He tried to keep his voice level when all he wanted to do was break down the door and drag Charles Winston out by his turnaround collar. "Emily Peacock gave me your address."

There was silence for a moment, then a harsh buzzer sounded. Hunter pushed open the front door and ran up two flights of stairs rather than wait for the dilapidated elevator. 3B was on the left hand side of the hallway. He rapped his knuckles against it, and the door cracked opened only as far as the privacy chain would allow.

A balding man peeked out. "ID, please."

Hunter swallowed his impatience and whipped out his badge, holding it to the crack. "I need to speak with you. It's an emergency."

Winston closed the door and Hunter heard the chain rattle before it opened again. Charles Winston was a short, slight man of perhaps fifty, who barely reached Hunter's shoulder. He didn't look much like a priest to Hunter, dressed as he was in a pair of frayed black pants, a blue pullover sweater, and worn Keds.

He stepped aside for Hunter to enter the apartment. "What's this about, Detective? How do you know Emily Peacock?"

Hunter stood in the middle of the living room as Winston closed the door and turned to face him. The ex-priest lived frugally; that was immediately apparent in the few sticks of furniture and tattered lace window coverings. "I need your help getting rid of a ghost," Hunter said.

Winston eyeballed Hunter for a long moment. "Tell me."

He breathed a sigh of relief that Winston hadn't dismissed him out of hand as a whack job, and gave Winston an abbreviated version of the events, up to Gant's murder of Emma Weils and abduction of Cooper. The story sounded ludicrous to Hunter's ears even though he knew every word of it was true. He bit his lip, waiting for Winston's reaction.

"You must understand how skeptical I must be of stories such as these," Winston said. "The only reason I am still listening is because Emily Peacock gave you my name. She would not have done so if you were exaggerating, or mistaken about the source of your problems."

"It's true, I swear it! Listen, Father, We don't have any time to lose. Gant has Cooper right now, and God knows what he's doing to the boy. We think he's taken the boy aboard the *Mary Gray*. My partner is there trying to keep Gant from hurting Cooper, but I need you to help me send the bastard to hell where he belongs before he kills another innocent person!"

Winston held up a hand. "I haven't been a priest for years, Detective. My views on demonology and exorcisms were in direct conflict with the teachings of the Church. They excommunicated me, threw me out on my rosy-red, Irish cassock."

"I don't care. If you can help me, then I need you!"

Winston folded his hands behind his back and began to pace. "You must understand, Detective. Exorcisms are risky in the best of circumstances. In most instances, it is a person at the center of the exorcism, possessed by a demon or the ghost of a former living soul. The rites are performed to rid the body of the intruding spirit. I've had occasion to experience many house hauntings as well, but neither is the case here. I'm not even sure if the rites would work."

"We have to try. I'm out of options!"

"I understand your desire to protect the boy, Detective, but performing an exorcism such as you suggest is dangerous to everyone involved, including the child. If we do nothing, the boy may die but his soul will be free and remanded to heaven. If we fail, the boy will likely die anyway, and your ghost may become more powerful than ever. Even if we *succeed*, the child -- you said his name is Cooper? -- may die in the process, and both Cooper's soul and your friend David's may become so entangled with the killer's that they are dragged into hell along with him. Which outcome would you prefer, Detective?"

Hunter sputtered in outrage. "I'd prefer Cooper to stay alive!"

"As would I, of course. I am only making you aware of the possibilities. Exorcisms are never to be entered into lightly, and once begun they must be seen through to a conclusion no matter the outcome. Even your soul, your *life* may be at risk, Detective. Are you ready to accept that all may not go as you wish? Can you live with the consequences if it goes badly?"

Hunter balled his fists, jamming them into his thighs, wanting nothing more than to grab Winston and throttle him, force him to agree. He fought his anger down, although it was difficult. When he spoke, it was through clenched teeth. "I can't sit by and let that bastard kill Cooper. I have to do something, anything! If you won't help me, I'll try to do it myself."

Winston looked shocked, and for the first time, truly afraid. "No! You mustn't, Detective. Don't even consider such foolishness! You don't know what you're saying…in trying to rid yourself of one ghost, you might unleash demons that will make your killer look like a Boy Scout. Or, you may be pulled beyond the veil body and soul. If that happens, may God have pity on you. You'll be trapped there forever."

"Then you'll help me?"

Winston seemed to deflate, as if an invisible fist squeezed all the air out of him. He nodded. "I seem to have no choice in the matter, now do I? Not if I want to save you from your own foolishness." His blue eyes grew hard and he glared at Hunter. "Understand this, Detective: when I begin the rites, you are not to interfere, no matter what happens. To do so is to invite calamity. Do I have your word?"

"Sure, sure, whatever you say. Just hurry up, please! We have to get to the *Mary Gray* before Gant hurts Cooper!" Hunter replied. Or David, he added mentally.

"Then I'll get my equipment, and God help us all," Winston said. He crossed himself and walked out of the room.

When he returned, he held a small black bag that reminded Hunter of a doctor's kit. He wore a turnaround priest's collar, and a purple silk stole over his shoulders. Hunter cocked an eyebrow at him. "I thought you weren't a priest anymore?"

"It's simply window dressing, Detective, nothing more. If your ghost was once a Catholic, or is at least aware of the dogma of the Catholic faith, seeing me in priest's garb may lend weight to the rites. In truth, it isn't the clothing that makes the exorcist successful, but the faith of the one being excised. If your ghost was an atheist, no amount of prayer or dogmatic rites will persuade him to leave. To the atheist, an exorcism would be no more than a mouth load of drivel. Not only do *I* have to believe in order for it to be effective, Detective…so does he."

Hunter swallowed hard and found himself hoping Gant had been a religious man while alive. "My car is outside."

* * * * *

Hunter was silent on the drive to the *Mary Gray*. He drove on instinct, his mind a whirlwind of questions. What if Gant didn't believe in the rites? What if the exorcism didn't work? What if something went wrong? Cooper might die. David might be dragged into hell. Gant might remain, more powerful than ever. What was he getting himself into?

He almost decided to turn around, to take Winston back to the apartment. The risk is too great, he told himself. *It probably won't work anyway, and even if it does, I can't take the chance that something might go wrong. I'm sorry for Cooper, but I have to think of David. I can't lose him!* Then he was ashamed of his selfish and cowardly thoughts. David wouldn't turn back. David would charge ahead, both barrels blazing.

But he wasn't David. He was just a man, one who'd recently found something that gave meaning to his life, one that rekindled the will to live he lost ten years ago with David's death, and that he'd thought he'd never find again.

It was only the ghost of David's voice in his head that kept his foot on the accelerator. *Hunter, stop being an idiot. We* have *to do this. It's our job.*

Well, fuck, Hunter thought petulantly. *Maybe I should start thinking about changing jobs. Become a security guard maybe, or a janitor, or write a fucking cookbook. Anything that doesn't require putting the man I love in jeopardy.*

Pussy, David said in his mind.

Hunter ground his molars at the imagined taunt and kept driving.

He pulled up to the dock at which the *Mary Gray* sat anchored. The sight of the ship filled him with dread; the rusting black iron looked like the gateway to hell to him. He fought back a shiver as he got out of the car and led Winston to the gangplank.

"There are no other living souls about, I take it?" Winston whispered as they made their way up the gangway.

"Not to my knowledge. The ship is used as a storage facility. My partner said no one has been aboard in months. Well, nobody alive, anyway."

"Good. The fewer living souls at risk, the better." Winston's expression was strained but committed.

Hunter suppressed another shudder and pushed at the heavy door at the head of the gangway. It slid open with a long, metallic creak that sounded like a scream. It was very dark inside, the only light filtering through filthy portholes.

"David?" Hunter whispered. "Where are you?"

He heard David's voice in his head. *"In Gant's cabin, Hunter!"*

Suddenly, a man appeared in front of Hunter. He was older, and his throat had been slashed. Hunter quickly realized he was a ghost. "You best follow me. I'll bring ye down right quickly enough. Bastard has the boy."

"Who are you?" Hunter asked.

"Who are you talking to?" Winston asked.

"A ghost," Hunter replied to Winston. He signaled for Winston to keep silent, keeping his eyes on the specter. "Who are you?"

"Me name is Abe. I be a friend of that other constable, the one what came looking for Gant." Abe turned away, floating farther into the ship, and motioned for Hunter to follow. "Best hurry. No telling what that bastard might be up to now."

"Go with him, Hunter," David's voice said in his mind. Hunter might not know this Abe ghost, but he trusted David. He followed along, with Winston keeping close to his heels.

Abe led them down two rusting flights of narrow, metal stairs to a long hallway. Rounded doorways lined the hall, but Abe bypassed them all until he nearly reached the end, then pointed to the door on the left. "In there, he be. I hope ye send him to hell, laddies, and may he rot there for eternity." With that, Abe disappeared, leaving Hunter and Winston alone in the hall.

"Hunter? Are we…alone?" Winston asked softly.

Hunter nodded and gestured toward the door. "They're in here," he said. "Are you ready?"

Winston lifted a large cross, hanging from his neck by a thin gold chain, to his lips, and kissed it. He let it fall again, then opened the battered black book he held to a bookmarked page. He shoved a hand into his pocket and withdrew a small plastic bottle with a black cross on it.

Holy water, Hunter presumed. He wondered if Winston's theory that the spirit needed to believe in its power for an exorcism to work also held true for holy water. David had told him Gant confessed that the holy water had hurt him, so it seemed likely Gant believed in the holy water's power. At least, he hoped so.

He felt slightly better about the whole damn plan as he pushed open the door and stepped inside the cabin.

David was standing in front of a bunk, facing off against Gant. Cooper sat on the bunk behind David, looking very small and very pale. It must be astral-Cooper, Hunter thought. *I can practically see through him. It's not his physical body sitting there.* He pushed the wonder of it aside. He didn't have time to contemplate the laws of physics or lack thereof; he needed to concentrate.

"Oh ho! Look who's joined the party!" Gant sneered. "Just in time to see me rip out the boy's spine!" He took a step toward David.

Hunter tried to control his emotions. He didn't want to give Gant the fuel Gant needed to hurt either David or Cooper, but it was so fucking hard! He wanted nothing more than to strangle Gant with his bare hands. From behind him, Hunter heard a soft voice murmuring in Latin. Winston had begun the exorcism.

Then Gant laughed, the maniacal sound breaking Hunter's concentration. "Nothing can stop me. Not you, and not this fucking ghost, and not your priest." In his hand, he held a length of rusty chain. "I'm going to kill the boy. Then I'm going to kill you and the priest."

Hunter felt his anger slip from his control. He began to shake, trying to reel it back in, to calm himself, but couldn't. He watched in horror as Gant swept David aside and went after Cooper. He knew instinctively that Gant was hitching on his rage. If they didn't stop him, Gant would kill Cooper!

Winston stepped around Hunter, chanting faster. His arm whipped forward, flinging holy water at Gant. "Leave this child in peace!" he cried in a voice stronger than Hunter might have imagined the slight man to command. As impossible as it sounded, Hunter thought he heard more than one voice issue from Winston's mouth. "The power of Christ compels you!"

The wall behind Gant looked odd, strange enough to almost take Hunter's attention away from Gant. It no longer looked solid; instead it reminded Hunter of the surface of a deep, dark pond. Had Winston's rite summoned it up? What was it? Was it real, or was he imagining it?

It's the veil, Hunter thought with sudden insight. *The membrane that separates the living from the dead. I thought it would be brighter, more welcoming, not battleship gray.*

Gant screamed, redirecting Hunter's attention. Gant ducked away from the spray of holy water. He lifted his face, bellowing at the ceiling. An arm snaked out, grabbing Winston by his turnaround collar. With one powerful swing, Gant flung Winston into the wall. Winston crumpled to the floor in a heap, silent. His bottle of holy water lay next to him, the contents spilled.

Hunter stared, frozen in place. In all the scenarios that had gone through his head about how the exorcism might end, this had not been one of them. He couldn't even take the time to see if Winston was still alive. His attention was riveted on Gant as Gant advanced again toward Cooper. What were they going to do now?

He saw David moving from the corner of his eye, advancing on Gant. *No! Stay away, David! I can't lose you!*

Was this it then? Was this how it was going to end? Was Gant going to win? Hunter knew in his bones that Gant would kill Cooper and send David's ghost into whatever lay beyond the veil if Gant was allowed to reach them. Hunter roared, fury surging through his blood. Lowering his head, he charged toward Gant.

The room, a study in tightly strung tension a moment before, seemed to explode with movement. One moment David was holding his own, keeping Gant at arm's length and away from Cooper, and the next, he felt a surge of rage whip through the room like a whirlwind. He blinked, and suddenly there was a strange man lying crumpled on the floor and Hunter was running full-tilt toward Gant.

Everything seemed to freeze in place then, the world slowing to a crawl as David saw and felt everything all at once.

Gant was screaming, holding his face in his hands as if in pain. The man on the floor was conscious and muttering in a language that sounded -- as far as David could tell, since he'd never had an ear for languages even while alive -- like Latin, and Hunter...well, Hunter was a ball of fury, fairly *sizzling* with rage.

David couldn't help but hitch on the strong emotions churning through Hunter. Like a movie run at fast-forward, David saw and felt every frustration, every fear, every moment of anger Hunter had been chewing on since the first time the Weapon of Opportunity Killer had struck. He again felt Hunter's grief over David's death, frustration over David's appearance as a ghost. He tasted Hunter's fury at Bobby Weils, and anguish over Emma Weils' death. David felt Hunter's rage at Gant anew, his disappointment that the exorcism, their last ditch attempt at ridding the world of Gant, had seemingly failed, and fear for Cooper's life. Underlying it all, he felt Hunter's deep love for him, and an unspoken dread that David might one day disappear forever. All these emotions and more surged through him, electrifying him.

Something was happening else was happening. David noticed through his growing red haze of fury the appearance of a grayish, swirling mass on the far wall of the room. He'd never seen anything like it before. Semi-opaque -- he could still see the wall through it -- it also seemed to have a great depth to it, like a tunnel.

A tunnel.

The tunnel!

He realized that the exorcism was working, at least partially. Somehow, the priest had managed to open some sort of gateway between this world and the next, although Gant didn't seem to be moving toward the grayish mass. Perhaps the priest was too weak, or too injured, or Gant was too strong for the mumbled prayers to force Gant into it.

Hunter was moving, he realized, running at Gant. In an instant, David realized Hunter's intention. Hunter was going to sacrifice himself by pulling Gant into that swirling gray whirlpool and into the next world.

He felt a bellow begin deep in his gut, and when he opened his mouth a full-bellied roar rolled through the room. With one last look at Hunter that was filled with every ounce of the love David felt, he threw himself at Gant, reaching him only a heartbeat or two before Hunter could. Fueled by Hunter's emotions, he tackled Gant in a full-body slam that would've surely broken bones had they been alive, and propelled them both into the churning vortex.

Chapter Twenty-one

There was no sound, no feeling, nothing but blackness -- no eyes or ears, for that matter. There were no smells, no tastes. The universe was a vacuum, and he was completely numb. For perhaps the first time in his existence, he truly felt *dead*. Then even that fleeting impression was gone.

One moment he had been consumed with rage, burning with it, and the next, he felt like an empty husk, completely drained; floating in blackness so complete that he couldn't tell where he ended and the darkness began. Soon, even his dim memories of the negative emotions he'd been engulfed by faded away, leaving only peace behind.

The blackness was soothing, cradling him like the dark waters of a tropical sea, rocking him. He could be content to float there forever. He felt a natural part of the darkness, as if he were born to it; it surrounded him and permeated him to his core.

After what seemed to him to be a long while but might have been only seconds -- time did not exist in this nothingness -- he noticed a pinpoint of light off in the distance that was twinkling in an oddly appealing way, although *how* he saw it without the benefit of eyes was beyond him. It just *was*, the way you knew air existed without having to see it. He felt the strongest urge to go to the light; it sang a strange, seductive siren's song that was felt rather than heard, but he fought to ignore the compulsion. He wanted to stay where he was, bobbing gently in the arms of the night.

His thoughts wandered, tripping and stuttering over various bits and pieces that might be memories but seemed too removed to be his own. He thought he remembered feeling strongly, fear and hate and rage, although if he did, he didn't know why. The emotions were like ghosts, barely glimpsed out of the corner of his eye. They no longer touched him, no longer held any power over him. What had he been doing? He couldn't remember. His memories danced out of reach and he gladly let them go.

The light was closer now, larger, no longer a pinpoint but rather like a spotlight on a stage. It was not simply light, but *Light*, powerful and compelling and full of promise. Instead of feeling nothing at all, he could feel its distant heat, weak but holding the promise of warmth, like the sun on a cold winter's day. In his mind it was diamond-white, yet seemed speckled with beautiful colors. How odd. It seemed to be pulling him slowly but inexorably toward it. He wondered what the Light was, what lay inside it, and why it wanted him.

A name flared briefly in his mind. His name, David. David…something. Never mind, it would come to him.

He set his thoughts free again, and a man's face suddenly flickered in his mind's eye for a moment, distorted and blurry, before disappearing again. He had the strangest feeling the face was important to him for some reason, and concentrated, trying to bring it back into focus. Slowly, like puzzle pieces sliding into place, it did. Blue eyes, crystalline, piercing. Dark hair. A strong jaw. A smile for the angels. Hands, a mouth, a body that could give pleasure so sharp it bordered on pain.

Another name flittered through his mind, this one sounding soft and reverential, like a prayer.

Hunter.

With the name came a powerful memory, sharp and crisp, of a love he once felt associated with the name. In the absence of any other emotion it was razor sharp, slicing through him. It was so close to a physical sensation that it shocked him. His journey toward the Light slowed and stopped. He felt the pull of the Light, insistent now, demanding, but forced himself to ignore it, concentrating instead on the depth of the remembered love, of the warmth of it suffusing him to his marrow.

Hunter.

David had left him once before. He remembered that much now, although not why he'd gone or how. He also knew he'd returned to Hunter and stayed for a long while, but in the end had left Hunter again. Why? Why would he want to leave such an incredible love behind? Where was Hunter now?

He hadn't wanted to leave, he realized. He'd been forced to go, to save Hunter's life and the life of a small boy whose name and face he couldn't quite remember.

There was another man, tall and thin, but the memory of him dredged up black feelings of hate and fear. David pushed aside the memory of the hateful man, wanting to feel only the love he associated with Hunter.

The Light was pulling at him again, more forcefully now. It was as if the Light was alive, conscious, knew what David was thinking about, and was jealous of it. It was all David could do to resist it.

Hunter loved him, and he loved Hunter in return, he remembered that much now. An image of Hunter and himself naked in bed entered his mind. He remembered moments of potent ecstasy, and of feeling boneless and drained and happy. He remembered kisses, hard and punishing, and soft and sweet, and strong, calloused hands that nonetheless held a gentle touch.

Hunter was not in the blackness with him. Hunter had remained behind, wherever "behind" was, and had not followed David. For the first time since he became aware of himself floating in the darkness, David questioned if he wanted to remain there alone, without Hunter.

It was pleasant in the darkness, and the Light was incredibly seductive, but it suddenly all seemed very hollow without Hunter. It wasn't right. This wasn't the way it should be, the way David wanted it to be. He hadn't said good-bye, had he? No, everything had happened too fast.

What? What had happened?

His memories were coming faster now, stronger, more focused. He remembered his history with Hunter, their years as detectives and partners, and how he'd not wanted to admit to the feelings he had for Hunter.

When he remembered his death, all the pain and terror came back in a rush. He quickly moved past it, to when he returned to Hunter and finally, to the moment they realized they loved each other.

With those precious memories came the unpleasant ones about the killer, Gant, and David finally remembered how he'd come to be in the blackness. He'd sacrificed himself to save Hunter, to keep Hunter from touching Gant and being pulled through the gray mist and into death.

At one time David thought he needed to leave Hunter, to allow Hunter to find someone else, someone alive to share Hunter's life. Someone who could love Hunter, touch him without the need for hitchhiking on emotions.

David no longer believed that. He saw clearly now, understood for the first time that there was no one who could love Hunter as much as he did. They were meant for each other, fated to be together. Neither would ever be truly happy without the other.

It was then that something startling happened. He began to feel. Not ghostly, half-remembered emotions, but true, deep ones that sang through his bones like white lightning. They were painful, even the good ones. It had been so long since he'd felt any emotion other than those he'd hitchhiked on that he barely recognized them for what they were. Love, hate, fear, and a myriad of others, many so subtle, he had no name for them.

Alone in the black, his scream was heard only in his mind.

He felt himself jerked forward as if an invisible rope were tied to his innards, pulling him. It was the Light. The Light wanted him, was demanding he come to it. *Come to me,* it seemed to say. *I'll ease your pain, take it all away. I'll help you forget.*

He felt trapped, caught between the lure of the Light and his memories of Hunter. Both were incredibly strong, pulling him in opposite directions, and for a moment he thought he might be drawn and quartered, torn apart by them.

From somewhere in the depths of his soul, the stubbornness David had always fostered in life reared its head. He began to fight actively against the pull of the Light. Somehow he knew if he entered that brilliant Light, he would never be able to return to Hunter. The knowledge gave him strength, and he redoubled his efforts to pull away from it.

Slowly, infinitesimally, he began to inch backward, away from the Light. It was a struggle, one that forced him to use every scrap of energy he could muster. As the Light began to recede, his memories grew stronger yet, more detailed. He remembered his life with Hunter, his death, his return as a ghost. His memories of hitchhiking, of sex, of Cooper all returned, along with those of Gant, and the final fight that had landed him here in the blackness.

He knew where "here" was, at last. He was beyond the veil, the plane from which no soul returned.

Well, fuck *that.*

Light or no Light, veil or no veil, he was going back to Hunter even if it -- pardon the pun -- killed him.

Concentrating solely on Hunter, remembering Hunter's face, voice, and touch, grounded by his love for Hunter, David turned his symbolic back to the Light and began to move purposely through the darkness in the direction he'd come.

He found that going backward was exceedingly difficult. He felt as if he were swimming through quicksand. The blackness pushed back against him. It didn't want him to escape back to the land of the living anymore than the Light wished to release its hold on him. Every movement tested his resolve. It would be so easy to quit, to forget everything, and remain floating forever in the darkness, or better yet, to let the Light have him.

Only the memory of Hunter gave him the wherewithal he needed to continue. The only alternative was eternity without Hunter, and as far as David was concerned, that was no alternative at all.

I will not take the easy way out. I'm better than this, stronger. I will not *fucking lose!* The words repeated themselves over and over in his mind, a mantra that lent him strength. The words became another soundless scream as he wrenched away from the Light with all his being.

For moment he felt the blackness press against him like a solid, unyielding wall, and the pain of defying the Light was almost unbearable. Then suddenly, he felt himself push through the veil.

Streetlights, so harsh and cold and different from the Light, burned his eyes like an acid wash after the soothing darkness, and the heavy atmosphere of the living world made him feel as if he were buried alive under an invisible mountain, but it all faded quickly.

He looked around, and realized he was standing in front of Hunter's apartment building. It wasn't where he'd expected to be. He'd left Hunter aboard the *Mary Gray* with Cooper and the priest. David tried to figure out how long he'd been gone, but he couldn't be certain. Time moved differently beyond the veil.

He decided he'd check Hunter's apartment, and if Hunter wasn't there, David would go back to the *Mary Gray*. It took only a moment for him to remember how to fold space, and he hurriedly navigated the fluff of it to reach Hunter's living room.

To his relief, Hunter was there, but the reaction he got when Hunter saw him was a far cry from what he'd expected.

"What the fuck are *you* doing here?" Hunter gasped.

Before David could answer, Hunter keeled over in a dead faint.

Chapter Twenty-two

Hunter blinked awake slowly. He became aware that he was on the floor, and that he must've blacked out, hitting his head on his way down. He had a fierce headache, and when he gingerly reached up his fingers, he touched a knot on his forehead.

"Jeez, I would think you'd be happy to see me."

Hunter felt his eyes grow wide. He rubbed them, wondering -- no, *hoping* he'd jarred something loose inside his noggin when he'd hit his head. He must have, because that couldn't *possibly* be David standing in Hunter's living room. It couldn't be. David was dead. Again, and for good this time.

Or so Hunter had thought up until two minutes ago.

"No," he said, shaking his head and instantly regretting it when the movements made his skull throb painfully. "No, no, no! You are *so* not doing this to me again, David. You're fucking dead. Act like it!"

David stared at him. "What are you talking about? I'm not stupid. I know I'm dead, but you don't need to continually throw it up in my face. It certainly didn't bother you before. What's wrong with you?"

Hunter sputtered, dragging himself to his feet. "What's *wrong* with me? Oh let's see…how about the fact that I fucking buried you *twice?* Huh? Once wasn't bad enough. Oh no. You had to come back and make me fucking fall in love with your sorry ass, and then go and die on me *again*. And then you come back -- *again* -- and have the balls to ask what's wrong with me?" His voice kept rising in pitch until it squeaked near the end of his tirade, but he didn't care. How could this be happening to him? He couldn't deal with it. He couldn't. He wouldn't. He turned his back on David, as if not seeing him would negate David's presence.

He couldn't block his ears, though, and heard confusion in David's voice. "What are you talking about, Hunter? I was only gone a few minutes. An hour, at most. I almost didn't come up here because I figured you'd still be aboard the *Mary Gray*."

Hunter spun around and glared at David. "A few *minutes?* Don't play games with me. I deserve better than that. You've been gone almost a fucking *year*, David. Three hundred and sixty days, to be exact."

David gaped at him, no doubt picking up on the incredulity Hunter was feeling. "That's impossible!"

His expression seemed genuine, though, and it gave Hunter pause. David looked every bit as shocked as Hunter had felt when David appeared in the living room. He knew it couldn't be, though. David was a ghost, and ghosts didn't have emotions of their own. "Check the fucking calendar if you don't believe me." Hunter motioned toward the kitchen, where he always kept one pinned to the wall next to the phone. It was filled with appointments and phone numbers.

He'd always found it easier to use than a datebook, or God forbid, a Blackberry. He followed behind David, rapping his knuckles under the year at the top of the calendar. "See? Almost an entire fucking year, gone! Where were you, David? How could you do that to me?"

"I...I didn't do it on purpose! I mean, I did, but I had no choice. I was trying to save your fucking life!" David said. His face was a thunderous black cloud.

Hunter inadvertently took a step backward. He was angry, sure, but not that angry. He was feeling more hurt than pissed off. How was David channeling the rage he saw in David's face? "W-what are you talking about?"

"You were going for Gant, Hunter. If you managed to make contact with him, he might have sucked you into hell. I couldn't let that happen. I was already dead...I figured what would it hurt? I had nothing left to lose. I didn't know I'd get stuck there, or be gone so long. I still can't believe it. A whole fucking *year?* Holy shit. It only felt like a few minutes to me." David began to pace, taking short, angry strides.

No, it must be his imagination. It was impossible for David to feel anything. It's probably the shock of seeing him again, he thought. Hunter thrust his fingers through his hair, wincing when they hit the bump on his forehead, and blew out a frustrated breath. He slumped onto a kitchen chair. "I can't keep doing this, David. I can't keep burying you. You don't know what it was like. I kept hoping you were going to show up again, but you never did. Every day I'd wake up hopeful, and go to bed devastated. It took me six months to accept the fact that you weren't coming back this time."

"But I *did* come back."

"Sure you did...a year later!"

"Well, pardon me. I'm so sorry I'm late," David said sarcastically. "I was a little busy being dead and all and trying to move heaven and earth to come back to you. You know, there's a reason nobody who's gone beyond the veil has ever come back. It ain't exactly easy."

"Neither is burying the man you love twice!"

"Will you *please* stop saying that? You're killing me here."

Hunter felt his blood pressure inch up a notch. He was no longer upset…he was furious. He jumped to his feet, ignoring the way the movement made his head pound. "Is that supposed to be funny?"

David's eyes snapped fire. "No. It's tragic. You said you loved me, but instead of being happy to see me, you're giving me grief about being gone so long! Would you rather I stayed away? I can do that, you know. I can go back."

The words were like a knife stabbed directly into Hunter's heart. His chest seized so suddenly he could barely breathe. "Don't you fucking even think about it!" The dam broke. All the pain and sorrow he'd been keeping bottled up deep inside came flooding out, and he collapsed on a kitchen chair, his legs too wobbly to hold him upright any longer. He swiped at his eyes angrily, embarrassed at his loss of control. "Jesus, David…I wanted to die. Honestly, I just wanted to find a hole and bury myself in it. If it wasn't for Cooper, I think I might've done it."

"Cooper? Is he okay? What happened after I took out Gant?" David knelt next to Hunter, one hand on his knee. It took Hunter a minute to realize he could feel David's hand, warm and strong, and another to realize how much he'd missed David's touch.

"Coop's fine. After you disappeared with Gant, the swirly gate-thing or whatever it was that Winston opened up closed again. Winston said Gant was gone for good…and so were you."

A broad smile lit David's face. "Thank God. It worked! Man, that makes what I went through worth it." David's hand lifted to cup Hunter's chin. "*You* make it worth it, Hunter. I couldn't face an eternity without you. I would've walked through fire to get back here if that's what it took. I'm only sorry it took so long."

Hunter blinked, and covered David's hand with his own, then slowly peeled it away from his face. A new worry reared briefly. If David could find a way back, what if Gant could too? He pushed it away. No sense in worrying about something he had no control over. He cocked his head, eyeing David. "Something's different about you," he said. "You've changed somehow."

Another bright smile creased David's cheeks. "I found out a secret while I was in there, Hunter, or out there, or wherever 'there' is. It's not that ghosts can't feel emotions...it's that ghosts don't *want* to feel them."

"What?"

"When you're alive, your spirit, your essence, whatever you want to call it, is protected by your body. It's encapsulated, surrounded by flesh and bone. Emotions can't hurt it. Oh, they can be painful, but not deadly.

"But when you die and your body is suddenly gone, emotions feel like bullets ripping through you. Ghosts can't handle it -- and like I've said before, there's no instruction manual to tell them how. They shut that part of themselves off. Not intentionally; it's more of an instinctive thing, done automatically, like holding your breath when you go underwater. Most spirits cross through the veil immediately and go into the Light, and never have to worry about it anymore. The ones who stay behind don't question their ability to feel. I never did. I learned to hitchhike, and thought that was as good as it was going to get. I think there were a few times when I was close to feeling emotions for myself, but I didn't want to believe it, and pushed them away. And

I did love you, although I never quite put it down to feeling emotions. For some reason, I always thought it was different, or just a reflection of what you felt for me."

David's arms wrapped around Hunter, and held him close. Hunter could feel the bulge of David's biceps pressing almost painfully around him. "But here's the kicker -- it doesn't have to be that way. I can feel now, Hunter. Really *feel*. I was actually angry before when you were giving me a hard time about coming back. I was happy when you told me Cooper is okay, and I felt sad because I hurt you, even if it was unintentional. Most of all, I love you. Really love you, with all my heart and soul."

Hunter slipped his arms around David, reveling in how real David felt, how solid. "What does all this mean?"

"It means we can be together whenever we want. It means I can do *this* whenever I want," David said. His kiss was softer and sweeter than any Hunter could remember, yet filled with the promise of a passion so fiery it scalded Hunter's soul.

David pulled away a bit, looking hard at Hunter. "I'm not going to lie to you, Hunter. I'm still dead. A ghost. Nobody else can see me or hear me. Life won't be easy for you. We can't go to dinner or a movie without it appearing that you're going solo. You can't take me to the Policeman's Ball as your date. We can't open a bank account together or buy a house. You'll still have to pretend to be talking on the phone when you speak to me in public, so people won't think you're crazy."

Hunter barked a short laugh. "So I'll wear a Bluetooth earpiece, and I never liked going to those stupid balls anyway. Shit, David, is this for real or am I fucking dreaming?"

"Oh, it's for real, lover." David waggled his eyebrows at Hunter. "First thing I plan on doing is taking you to bed and fucking you into the mattress. Then, when we're done, we're going to do it again. I've got ten years of loving to catch up on. You may not sleep for a year."

This time Hunter's laugh was full and unrestrained. "Sounds like a plan to me." Then his smile faded a little. "The sex may have to wait a little while longer yet. You're wrong, David. There *is* someone else who can see and hear you, and he should be home from school any minute. The bus drops him off right outside the building."

David raised an eyebrow. "What are you talking about? You mean *Cooper?* What's he doing here?" Understanding suddenly flared in David's eyes. "Oh my God. You mean you...?"

"Who else would do it? Cooper is a special needs child -- more special than anybody at DCF could ever realize. His mom was gone and his dad is in prison, not that his dad was any good to Coop before getting sent away. He was all alone, and he needed me, David. I went through the all steps and became his foster dad. Having Cooper was what kept me sane after you left. I'm considering adopting him. Are you cool with this?" Hunter held his breath, wondering what in the blue fuck he would do if David wasn't good with it.

David's expression looked stunned for a moment, then his face split into a wide, delighted grin. He jumped up, both hands planted on top of his head. "Are you kidding me? I like Cooper, always did. He's a great kid. Wow, I never thought I'd be a dad. This is so fucking unbelievable, Hunter! I have two people I can talk to now! And yes, you have to adopt him. Absolutely."

Hunter felt a wash of relief, and stood up, reaching for David. They met in a sloppy, wet kiss that lasted until they heard the front door open and close.

"I'm home!" a childish, singsong voice proclaimed.

David's eyes flashed open wide. "Is that...he's talking? Outloud?"

"Cooper, yes. I had him enrolled in the school Emma told us about, the one she couldn't afford. He's been doing great. He's talking now, and not living inside his head as much. He's really starting to open up to me, David."

David looked at Hunter, still smiling. "Wow. Cooper's home. And so am I."

What a family -- a ghost lover and a psychic, astral-projecting son, Hunter thought. He grinned as he led David into the living room to greet Cooper. *Perfect. Just perfect.*

And it was.